Hank THE COWDOG®

FADED LOVE

· John R. Erickson ·

Illustrations by Gerald L. Holmes

Maverick Books
Published by Gulf Publishing Company
Houston, Texas

Maverick Books
Published by Gulf Publishing Company
P.O. Box 2608 Houston, Texas 77252-2608

10   9   8   7   6   5

Library of Congress Cataloging-in-Publication Data
Erickson, John R., 1943–
      [Hank the Cowdog and faded love]
      Faded love/John R. Erickson: illustrations by Gerald L.
Holmes.
          p.   cm.—(Hank the Cowdog; #5)
      Originally published: Hank the Cowdog and faded love.
      Summary: Hank the Cowdog quits his job as Head of
Ranch Security and travels in search of adventure and
romance.
      ISBN 0-87719-064-X.—ISBN 0-87719-136-0 (pbk.).—
ISBN 0-87719-137-9 (cassette)
      1. Dogs—Fiction. [1. Dogs—Fiction. 2. West (U.S.)—
Fiction. 3. Humorous stories.] I. Holmes, Gerald L., ill. II.
Title. III. Series: Erickson, John R., 1943–   Hank the Cow-
dog; #5.
      [PS3555.R428H278 1991]
      813´.54—dc20
      [Fic]   91-2969
                                                                  CIP
                                                                  AC

Printed in the United States of America

Cover design by Tom Hair

Hank the Cowdog is a registered trademark of
John R. Erickson

Contents

Have you read all of Hank's adventures?
Available in paperback at $6.95:

All books are available on audio cassette too!
($15.95 for two cassettes)

Also available on cassettes:
Hank the Cowdog's Greatest Hits!

CHAPTER

1

THE CASE OF THE GIANT RATTLESNAKE

I t's me again, Hank the Cowdog. It was your normal, average, run-of-the-mill spring afternoon on the ranch—until Drover brought the news that Sally May's baby was being attacked by a *giant rattlesnake.*

And suddenly it became un-normal, un-average, and un-run-of-the-mill.

I was up by the chicken house, as I recall, taking testimony from J. T. Cluck, the head rooster. He had reported "strange sounds in the night." I had gone up to check it out.

"All right, J. T., start at the beginning and tell me the whole story."

"You want the whole story?" He had a speech inpedamun—whatever you call it when a guy whistles all his S's. Speech unpedamin.

1

"That's correct. And remember: tiny details are often the most important. And try not to whistle."

"All right, Hank. This thing has me worried. Elsa says I worry too much. Only last week she told me . . ."

"Wait a minute. Is that the beginning?"

He stared at me and blinked his eyes. "Oh. You want me to start at the beginning, you say?"

"Let's try it that way and see how it works."

"All right." He rolled his right wing around in its socket. I took careful note of the movement, knowing that it might turn out to be an important clue. "Derned wing's been giving me fits."

"Hold up. Was it bothering you before you heard the strange noise in the night or after?"

"Huh? What are you talking about?"

"Strange noise in the night."

"Oh, that. No, has nothing to do with it. This sore wing's been coming on for six months, maybe a year. Elsa says . . ."

"Let's get on with the story."

"Okay, here we go." He closed his eyes and concentrated. Then the eyes popped open. He glanced over his shoulder, leaned toward me, and whispered, "You know what bothers me

2

most about this whole darned thing?''

"What?"

"What bothers me most about this whole thing is the way these darned kids act. If you ask me, we've raised up a whole generation of ungrateful chickens that don't know manners. And you want to know what else I think?''

"No."

3

His beak froze open. "Huh?"

"No. I didn't come up here for your latest sermon. Just give me the facts about a strange noise in the night."

"Oh. Well, I was a-getting to it, but yes, we definitely had a strange noise in the night. Very strange, Hank. It must have been close to dark, see, and we'd gone to roost and the chicken house had got real quiet and still."

"All right, go on."

"And you see them two little roosters over there?"

I looked to the right and saw them. I memorized their conformation. Actually, they looked like every other young rooster I'd ever seen: two wings, two legs, two feet, a lot of feathers, and a stupid expression. "Yes, I see them. Go on."

"Them's the laziest two boys that ever walked on this earth, and you know what else? They're MY boys! Now, how do you explain something like that?"

I was having a little trouble tying this all together. "What do the boys have to do with the strange noise?"

"I'm a-gettin' there. I remember waking up from a light sleep and saying to Elsa, 'Elsa, did you hear a strange noise?' And Elsa, she said she'd describe it as *peculiar,* not strange."

"Hmmmm."

"So we agreed, me and Elsa, that it was somewhere between strange and peculiar."

"Very good. Now you've got to concentrate. Do you have any idea what might have caused that kind of peculiar noise?"

Again, he looked around to see if anyone was listening, then leaned forward. "I've got a darned good idea, but first I need to know if you're the kind that's going to blab this all over the ranch."

"I didn't become Head of Ranch Security by blabbing."

"Okay. I just wanted to hear you say that before I gave you any more information."

"Go on, J. T. It's safe with me."

"Okay, I'll have to trust you. It was them two boys of mine. They'd been out playing around, see, and thought they could sneak back in while the old man was asleep."

I glared at him. "Wait a minute. I came up here to solve a mystery. Where is it?"

"Well, it's a mystery to me why their mother lets them boys get by with that kind of darned nonsense, and you always struck me as the kind of dog who cared about others and their problems, and it was kind of quiet this morning and I said to Elsa . . ."

I put my nose in his face and growled. "You're wasting my valuable time and I don't like that."

His beak dropped open. "Well there's no need to be tacky about it! If you want to know what I think . . ."

At that very moment, Drover came streaking up the hill, scattering hens and pullets in all directions. You should have seen the feathers fly! J. T. heard the commotion and started squawking.

"Help! Help! It's a wolf, run for your life!"

That was the last I saw of J. T. Cluck that day, which was just fine with me. There are very few things I hate worse than being suckered by a dumb chicken.

Drover arrived in a nervous spasm and a cloud of dust. "Oh Hank, come quick, you won't believe, oh my gosh, it's awful, help, attack, the baby, save him, Hank, it's all up to you!"

Ordinarily I would have told my assistant to calm down and give me the facts so I could build my case. I mean, there's such a thing as blind panic, and in this business you learn that blind panic is a poor place to start.

On the other hand, when duty calls, a loyal

cowdog must respond. I mean, answering the call of duty is just by George bred into us.

Did I stand around gathering facts, building my case, taking descriptions of suspects? Did I waste time asking Drover who was attacking what, where, when, and why? No sir. I lit a shuck and went streaking down the hill toward the gas tanks, scattering chickens.

"Out of the way, you fools!" You should have heard the squawking. Dumb birds.

I reached the gas tanks in a matter of seconds, stopped, set up a forward position, and waited for the enemy to show himself. He didn't appear, so I started barking.

"Hank!" Drover was standing at the top of the hill, in front of the house. "You went the wrong way. Up here!"

It appeared that I had . . . Drover's directions had been very vague. How was I supposed to . . .

I shot up the hill. "All right, where is he? Give me a coordinate."

"Left!"

I went streaking off to the left and heard Drover's voice again.

"Hank, not *your* left. MY *left*!"

I screeched to a halt, spun around, and sprinted back to Drover. "You're going to have to work on your navigation, son. This is unacceptable."

"I'm sorry, Hank, but I thought . . ."

"Never mind what you thought. Which way's the enemy?"

"In the yard. But you'll have to jump the fence."

In spite of the dangerousness and seriousness and emergenciness of the situation, I couldn't help smiling. "That fence means nothing to me, son. It's just one of life's many hurdles."

"Really? I don't think I can jump it."

"That's fine. Watch me and study your lessons."

"Okay, Hank. I'll work on it later."

"You bet you will—on your own time. Here I go!"

I got a run and virtually flew over that fence. A deer couldn't have done it better. I landed in the yard, went into my fighting crouch, set up a forward position, sniffed the air, and scouted the terrain.

The yard was Forbidden Territory, you might say. Sally May had planted grass and shrubs and flowers and other stuff, and Iron Law Number One on the ranch was that dogs weren't allowed inside the fence.

Cats were. You could usually find Pete the Barncat lolling around the back porch—waiting for a hand-out and never mind the rest, it makes me mad just thinking about the injustice of it.

Anyway, once inside Forbidden Territory, I scouted the terrain. Some thirty feet in front of me, I saw Little Alfred, Sally May and High Loper's baby boy. He was wearing a sailor's suit and playing with a dump truck.

A short distance from Little Alfred, perched upon a cardboard box, was a large cake with white icing and two yellow candles.

The clues were fitting together: baby, clean clothes, cake, candles. This was some kind of ceremony. An ordinary dog, untrained in security work, would have leaped to the conclusion that this was a birthday party. But, drawing on my years of experience, I didn't make that assumption. The facts said, "Ceremony of Some Kind," not necessarily a birthday party.

Two questions remained unanswered. First, *where was the child's mother?* And second, *what monster or evil force had put Little Alfred's life in danger?*

Those were the crucial questions in the case, and you'll notice that I had arrived at them only minutes after the first alarm. My next course of action was to search for some answers.

And I suspected Drover knew them.

CHAPTER

2

THE CASE TURNS OUT TO BE A PIECE OF CAKE

" "All right, Drover," I called out. "I'm ready to go into action. Two questions: Where is Sally May?"

"She went inside to get her camera."

"Number two: With whom or what do I go into combat?"

Drover swallowed hard. "Oh, Hank, I hate to tell you this. It's awful!"

"Nothing's awful unless you believe it's awful."

"You're going to be scared."

"I doubt that, son. Remember the Silver Monster Bird? Remember the Enormous Monster? Remember the night I defended the ranch against the entire coyote nation? With that

11

kind of combat record . . . never mind. Point me toward the enemy.''

His teeth were chattering. "Over by the baby. You want to know what it is?''

"Might as well.''

"It's a giant rattlesnake, Hank!''

"HUH?''

The hair stood up on the back of my neck. Chills rolled down my spine. All at once I felt the cold grip of fear closing around my throat.

I have very few weaknesses, very few clinks in my armor. In fact, you might say I have only one weakness: I'm scared of snakes, always have been. My Uncle Pottsy was bitten on the face by a rattlesnake and died a horrible death.

I started shaking. For a long time I couldn't speak. The only thing that kept me from losing control was Drover. It would have ruined him.

I fought against the shakes and chills, until at last I was able to speak. "One last question, Drover. Why didn't you handle this case by yourself? Why did you come get me?''

"Oh, I didn't think I could jump the fence. My leg's been . . .''

"Is that the only reason?''

"Uh huh. Oh, and I'm scared of snakes, especially rattlesnakes. They bite.''

"I see. Did it ever occur to you that I might be bitten?"

"No."

"Or that I might be afraid of snakes?"

"Oh heck no, 'cause you're not a chicken-hearted little mutt like me."

"That's true, unfortunately." I took a deep breath. "Well, I guess there's nothing left to say."

"No, just kill the snake and that'll be it."

I glanced over at Little Alfred, so innocent, so absorbed in his play. "Where'd you see the snake?"

"In the flowerbed, right behind the baby."

"Very well. So long, Drover."

"So long, Hankie. I'll be waiting right here."

"We can bet on that."

I turned and started walking toward my fate. It's funny, the memories that come back to you at such moments. I saw myself as a pup, playing tug-of-war with my sister Maggie while Ma watched us with a contented smile.

Seeing Ma that way kind of gave me courage. She's the one who taught me right from wrong, and I didn't want to disgrace her memory. My steps grew bolder and I marched up the flowerbed.

Little Alfred turned and smiled. "Goggie! Goggie!"

I dipped my head, as if to say, "How's it going, son?"

Then I turned to the grim task before me. I cocked my ear and listened. If the snake rattled, at least I would know his position and could plan my attack so that if I got bitten, it would be on the foot instead of the face. I wanted to save my face for . . .

Oh geeze, that started me thinking about Beulah again, my true and perfect collie love, the only woman in the world who could make me think of romance just before going into combat with a giant rattlesnake. But dang her soul, she loved a bird dog, and how could she love a bird dog . . .

I shook those thoughts out of my head. This was no time for romantic notions.

I cocked my ear and listened. Nothing. The snake wasn't going to give me any warning, which was a piece of bad luck. I had no choice but to sniff out the flowerbed and force the snake out into the open, offering myself as a target in order to save Little Alfred.

I was shaking again, and I mean all the way down to my toenails. I crept forward—sniff-

ing, listening, waiting for the ineffable . . .
uneffitable . . . inedible . . . whatever the dadgum word is, to occur. Inevitable.

Even though I was expecting a strike, it
shocked me when it came. I heard a hiss, saw
a blur of motion to my right, and felt a sting on
the end of my nose—the very worst and most
fatal place to take a snakebite.

I staggered back. My eyes began to dim. I felt
the poison rushing through my bloodstream.
My heart pounded in my ears. As I sank to my
knees, I uttered not a cry and faced my un-
timely end with the little shreds of courage I
could muster.

As the gray veil moved across my eyes, I
heard a strange voice: "Sorry about that,
Hankie. You woke me up and I thought you
were a big mouse."

HUH?

Hadn't I heard that whiny voice before?
That was no snake. That was Pete the Barncat!

I opened my eyes and sure enough, there
was Pete's insipid grin peeking out of the iris.
"What are you doing in there? I thought you
were a rattlesnake."

Pete licked his paw. "No, he was here but he
crawled under the house. Snakes are very

afraid of cats, you know, which is why a lot of
people think cats are better at ranch security
than dogs."

"Is that so?"

"Um hum. Because cats have something no
cowdog in history has ever possessed."

"Such as?"

He throwed an arch in his back, took a big
stretch, and scratched the ground with his
front paws. "Intelligence."

All at once I felt my energy coming back. I
stood up. "Oh yeah?"

"Um hum, and you can run along now,
Hankie, and . . . oh my goodness, your poor
little nose is bleeding!"

"Oh yeah? Well, that's real bad news for

you, cat, and here's what I'm going to do about it."

I went crashing into the iris patch, landed right in the middle of Pete, I mean, just buried him. He was going to pay dearly for his mistake. He'd drawn first blood and I was fixing to draw second blood—about two gallons of it.

I lifted one paw and waited to grab him with my teeth. He didn't come out. I lifted the other paw and . . . you might say that he'd slipped out of my trap.

Funny, how a cat can be right there in your clutches one second and gone the next. Makes a guy wonder how they do that, and I mean right there in front of your eyes. Beats me, but we can be sure that it saved Pete from a tragic and messy death, because Hank the Cowdog does not take trash off the cats.

I didn't have much time to study on Pete's escape, because just then Little Alfred came toddling over and got me in a headlock. He was still talking that "Goggie" stuff, which means "Heroic Guard Dog" in kid language.

Little Alfred may have been little, but he was built a lot like his old man, High Loper—plenty stout in the arms and shoulders. Kind of surprised me when he throwed that headlock on me and started dragging me around. Didn't figger a kid that age could do that, but he sure as thunder did.

And one of the first things that happened was that, all at once, I couldn't breathe. Little Alfred had got a good start on strangulating me.

Now, we need to get something straight right here. Your top-of-the-line, blue-ribbon, higher-bred cowdogs are famous for their incredible strength. As a group, we're probably the strongest breed of dogs ever known to

G.L.Holmes

mankind. I mean, shredding monsters, destroying obstacles, breaking into locked buildings—that's commonplace to us, just part of the job.

But what many people don't know is that, while we're licensed by the federal government as Dangerous and Lethal Weapons, we also have hearts of gold. We love children, and at an early age, we have to take a solemn oath never to bite or harm a child.

So here's the point. Anyone else who had throwed a headlock on me would have had tooth tracks over ninety percent of his body, and I mean within a matter of seconds. It's impossible to strangulate a cowdog without several winch lines and heavy equipment.

Unless it's done by an innocent child, and see, our Cowdog Oath forbids us from biting or scratching a child. So there I was, being dragged around the yard by Little Alfred and I couldn't get my wind and things was getting a little serious.

I just went limp and hoped for the best.

Just before he got me snuffed out, he let go and I dropped into the grass. I sat up and caught my wind and was beginning to think about making my exit before Sally May came back, when the little scoundrel ran his finger across the cake and put a big glob of icing in the front of my nose.

Ordinarily I'm not tempted by sweets. I've always figgered that too much sweets makes a dog soft. It ain't the hardship that ruins a good dog; it's the easy life.

On the other hand, we don't often get recognition in this line of work. We don't demand it, we don't expect it, we go on and do our job without it. But when it comes, a guy kind of hates to turn it down.

Here was this little fellow, offering me a small reward for a job well done. What could I do? I licked the icing off his finger. He got some more and, well, I took that too. Pretty good stuff. He kept dipping and I kept licking.

He really got a kick out of that. He was laughing and squealing and having a wonderful time. Here was a happy child. I knew Sally May wanted her child to be happy—wouldn't any mother?—so when Little Alfred stuck his whole hand into the cake and offered me a big hunk, I took that too—primarily out of a sense of duty.

I took a bite and he took a bite. Me and Little Alfred had become the best of friends, is what had happened. It was one of them unexpected magic moments when two of God's creatures sit down and share some of the good things in this life: friendship and cake.

I mean, we were different. We didn't speak the same language or come from the same stock, but all at once that didn't matter.

Seemed to me Little Alfred was working awful hard, digging that cake out with his hand and feeding me every bite, so I scootched a little closer to the box and showed him how to eat cake with no hands: just by George stick your face into it and go to lickin' and chewin'.

He loved that! And let me tell you, the kid was good at it. Well, we had our faces stuck in the cake and had just about eat the west side out of it, when all at once . . .

"Here I come, Sweetie. Daddy put the camera in the wrong place and the phone rang and . . . ALFRED! WHAT ON EARTH . . . HANK!!''

Huh? Our heads came up. I looked at Little Alfred and he looked at me. He giggled. I didn't. If I had anywhere near as much cake on my face as he did, fellers, I was in trouble.

It's hard to deny the crime when you're wearing the evidence.

Sally May's face turned red. She grabbed a rake and started toward us, in what you might call an angry walk. (Long, sharp steps.)

At a glance, I could see that this was going

to be another misunderstanding between me and Sally May. She didn't understand about the giant rattlesnake or me protecting her baby or the wonderful relationship me and Little Alfred had built up.

She probably thought I was in her yard, eating her cake. And she might have even suspected me of flattening her iris bed.

I hated to walk out on Little Alfred, but I had a pretty good idea which one of us was going to get the rake used on him. "YOU'VE RUINED MY CAKE, YOU, YOU, YOU HOUND!! GET OUT OF THIS YARD! AND MY FLOWERS!"

Just as I suspected.

I tucked my tail and started slinking away. When she throwed the rake at me, I slank no more. I ran.

I had solved The Case of the Giant Rattlesnake. You might even say it had been a piece of cake. But consider the price of success: my reputation was now in shambles.

ON THE ROAD AGAIN

Before I could get out of her yard, Sally May threw a hand trowel and Little Alfred's toy truck at me. She missed with both, but not by much. That truck would have hurt.

I vaulted the fence, right over the top of Drover. I could see his eyes. They were as big as two fried eggs in a skillet. I ran down the hill, past the gas tanks, and didn't slow down until I got to the sewer. By that time, Drover had caught up with me.

"Hank, what happened! Did you get the snake? Oh my gosh, what's that all over your face?"

I studied the runt for a minute. "One of these days I'm going to get tired of you sending me on suicide missions."

"What do you mean?"

"I mean there wasn't a snake in the flowerbed. It was a cat. Do you know the difference between a cat and a snake?"

"No, what?" He gave me that vacant stare of his.

"Just as I suspected. You saw Pete in the iris bed and somehow that little pea brain of yours made him into a giant rattlesnake."

"No, it was a rattlesnake, a huge one, and he was crawling right toward the baby. I know it was, Hank."

"All right, let's check that out. How many legs did your rattlesnake have?"

Drover rolled his eyes. "Well . . . not very many."

"How many ears?"

"Well . . . I didn't think to count 'em, Hank."

"By any chance did you hear the snake say 'meow' or 'mew'?"

"No, he didn't say a word."

"Was there anything on the end of his tail?"

"End of his tail. Well, if he was a rattlesnake, he must have had a rattle."

"But did you see it?"

"You'd think so, wouldn't you?"

"Uh huh. But did you see it?"

"If it was there, I saw it."

"You're being slippery, Drover, but I'm not easily fooled. Now, once again, *was it there*? What's your answer?"

"Can you give me a hint?"

"Either yes or no. Did you see a rattle on the end of his tail or not? It's very simple."

He thought for a long time. "Yes."

"Are you sure about that?"

"No. But you didn't say I had to be sure."

I sighed and shook my head. "Drover, you're the only dog in the security business whose testimony could be used by both sides at once."

"Thanks, Hank."

"That's no compliment."

"Oh gosh."

"I guess we'll never know if what you saw this morning was a snake or a cat or an elephant."

"It wasn't an elephant, Hank, I'm pretty sure about that."

"Are you trying to be funny?"

"Me? No."

"That's too bad. Just for a second there, I had a glimmer of hope." I waded out into the water and looked down at my reflection. My face was covered with cake crumbs and icing. I resembled a clown, which seemed very appropriate. "Drover, I'm a failure."

"You are?"

"I work eighteen hours a day on this place. I try to do the right thing, but it seems that every time I turn around, I'm in trouble again. It's just not worth it. Why, up there in the yard, I could have been killed by that rattlesnake."

"I thought it was a cat."

"And for what? Why do I go on, day after day, beating my head against a brick wall?"

"I bet that hurts."

"There's just no sense in it."

"Sounds crazy to me."

"Is it for the honor? The glory? The adventure?

"It's bound to be something."

"Drover, what do you think about love?"

"Oh, I'm for it."

"Maybe that's what's wrong with me. I've spent too many years wrapped up in my career and never took the time to fall in love. Sometimes a guy can't see the forest for the trees, Drover."

"Yeah, and most of 'em are down by the creek anyway."

"There's a whole world out there that I don't know anything about. It's a world of birds and butterflies and flowers."

"And hay fever."

"It's a world of sunshine and poetry and songs. Drover, do you think I'm too old to act silly again and fall in love?"

"I don't know, but you look pretty silly with that stuff all over your face."

I gazed at myself in the water. "Hank the Clown Dog, Head of Ranch Manurity. That's what I get for my years of service. You're right, Drover, it's time for a change. You've convinced me that it's time for old Hank to fall in love."

"I did that?"

"Yes. By being such an incredible dunce. By sending me on suicide missions. By proving over and over that chaos and mismanagement are the natural order of the universe."

"Gosh, thanks, Hank."

"Now, I shall take my bath and prepare this magnificent body for the ladies of the world. And then I'll bid farewell to this ungrateful place and travel down the creek to the next ranch, where dwells my true love."

Drover's ears shot up. "Hey, that's where *my* true love lives! I'll go with you."

"Very well, Drover, we'll go together, and together we'll embark on a new career."

"What career is that, Hank?"

I gave him a smile. "We're going to become troubadours, poets, and professional lovers."

"Boy, that sounds like fun."

"Yes, fun. What a strange word to me. I know so little about it. But I'll learn to be frivolous." I glanced up toward the house. "And one of these nights, when the moon is dark and the coyotes are slinking through the shadows, *they* will regret what they've done to me."

"Yeah, they'll be sorry."

What a delicious thought! Loper and Sally May, out with flashlights, calling my name, begging me to come back, promising a fresh start and a better deal. But too late.

I plunged into the warm green water, rolled and splashed and laughed and kicked my legs in the air. When I stepped out and shook myself, I felt as though I had washed away the old Hank and become a new dog.

Minutes later, we started off on our new adventure, heading down toward the creek. As we passed one of those big elm trees there in the flat, I caught a glimpse of Pete. He had seen us, and fearing for his life, he had begun slinking toward the tree.

The old Hank would have taken time to

G.L.Holmes

whip him and run him up the tree. But the new Hank considered him an irrelevance, just another bad memory from years of squandered youth.

"Don't bother to run, cat. I'm finished with you and this ranch. I'm a changed dog. I don't lower myself to chase cats any more."

He reached his claws up on the tree trunk and started sharpening them. "Oh really?"

"Yeah, really!" said Drover. "We're not kidding this time."

"I bet I can make you chase me," said Pete.

I laughed. "I'm beyond that, Pete, it's all behind me now. We're quitting this ranch forever. You can have it. It's yours."

He studied his claws. "I still bet I can make you chase me."

We stopped. "All right, go ahead. You'll find that I'm a changed dog. Try me." He humped up his back and hissed. "Nothing, Pete, sorry." He yowled and spit. I only laughed at him. He flicked the end of his tail back and forth. "The feeling's gone, Pete, sorry old boy."

Laughing at Pete and the whole ranch, Drover and I started out on our journey.

"How's your nose doing, Hankie?" That was Pete's voice.

I stopped. Slowly I turned my head until I could see him. He was sitting at the base of the tree, grinning and flicking the end of his tail.

"You shut your lousy rotten mouth about my nose!"

"Looks like somebody," he reached up and dragged his claws across the tree trunk, "scratched it."

"You've been warned, cat. One more word

out of you, and I'm liable to clean your plow.''

"Hmm. One more word? How about . . . NOSE!''

That did it. I went after him, and Drover was right behind me, saying, "Get 'im Hankie, get 'im!'' Derned near got him, but he managed to escape up the tree at the last possible second.

"And let that be a lesson to you, cat!'' I yelled at him.

He smiled and flicked his tail. "Told you I could make you chase me. You haven't changed so much.''

"That's what you think. We're leaving this ranch and we'll never be back.''

"Oh, you'll be back,'' said Pete. "I'll give you three days.''

CHAPTER

4

THE HORRIBLE QUICKSAND MONSTER

And so it was that Drover and I left the ranch forever, turned our backs on worry and responsibility, and went out into the big wide world to find our true loves.

We hit the creek just south of the house and followed it east through the home pasture. When we came to the Parnell water gap, Drover slipped under the fence and I stood there a moment, looking back.

"Goodbye, old ranch. We gave you our best for a lot of years, and that was more than you deserved. And on this spot we take a solemn oath, never to return."

I scooted under the fence and we continued our journey.

"That was real good, Hank, that stuff about the solemn oath."

"You liked that? Would you believe I just composed it on the spot?"

"No kidding? You mean, you didn't even have to think about it or anything?"

"No sir. It just by George popped out of my mouth."

We went on down the creek, and after a bit Drover said, "What happens if we decided we want to go back to the ranch?"

I gave him a sideward glance. "What happens is that we can't go back, ever, period."

"But we might change our minds."

"No, no, you don't understand solemn oaths, Drover. Once you've taken a solemn oath, you're bound to it for life. There's no turning back once you've taken an oath."

"Yeah, but what if we did turn back?"

"As far as I know, it's never been tested. We just don't know what might happen, but it would be very bad. Why do you ask?"

"Oh . . . I kind of miss the ranch."

"We just left the ranch!"

"I know, and that's about the time I started missing it."

"Well, shake it off and toughen up, 'cause we ain't going back."

"And I'm kind of hungry, too."

I stopped and glared at him. "Hungry! How can you be hungry at a time like this?"

"I don't know." He started crying. "But I'm hungry and I'm homesick and I want to go back to the ranch."

"I should have known better than to bring you along. You've got no guts, Drover, no backbone, no sense of adventure."

"I know it!" he blubbered. "I'm a failure, I've always been a failure. Can I go home now?"

"Sure, go on. You'd be doing me a big favor if you left right now, and the sooner the quicker."

He sniffed and wiped his eyes with a paw. "Thanks, Hank. You'll be better off without me."

"Indeed I will. You'll be sorry, of course, when I tell you about all my adventures."

"I know I will." He started slinking back toward the water gap. "Bye, Hank, and good luck."

"And good riddance to bad rubbish!"

He went his way and I went mine. I must have gone, oh, twenty or twenty-five paces when I had a change of heart. I hated for Drover to miss this opportunity. I mean, the little mutt had lived such a sheltered life, he needed a chance to widen his horizons.

I loped back to the west and caught up with him. "You feeling better now?"

"Yeah, now that I'm going home, I feel great . . . except I'm still hungry."

We'd just about reached the water gap by this time. "I'm feeling a little gant myself, Drover. Tell you what we're going to do. About a mile east of here, there's a low-water crossing. Let's me and you hot-foot it over there, and if you really want me to, I'll teach you how to live off the land."

"I never did that before."

"That's my whole point. See, what you don't know is that this world's just full of food—berries, roots, fish, wild game, you name it. And it's all out here, waiting for us to find it and eat it."

"Really?"

"Drover, once you've lived off the land, you'll never want another chunk of Co-op dog food."

"No fooling?"

"Trust me."

"And then can I go home?"

"Yes. We'll definitely take that under ad-

G.L.Holmes

visement at the proper time. Come on, let's go."

He hesitated and looked across the fence. "Well . . . it might be fun, and I sure am hungry."

"That's the spirit! Let's motivate."

We headed down the creek again, this time at a faster clip. I kept glancing over at Mr. Homesickness and expecting him to have another attack, but I guess he was thinking about food. When a guy thinks from his gut, it changes his whole attitude.

We reached the crossing along toward the middle of the afternoon. It was kind of a cement dam, see, with the country road going over the top, and there was a little pool of water backed up on the up-stream side.

When we walked up to the pool, we could see the perch and minnows swimming around.

"You see that, Drover? This creek is alive with food. It's everywhere! Our biggest problem is going to be trying to decide whether we want froglegs, minnows, crawdads, or fish for supper."

"I want a big fish."

"You want a big fish, by George we'll get you one. How big a fish you want?"

"Oh, three or four pounds ought to be plenty."

"A four-pounder be all right? Coming right up! Watch me and study your lessons."

I figgered the quickest way to teach the runt was to demonstrate. I mean, lectures and classroom stuff have their place, but there's no substitute for real-live, on-the-spot training.

I chose a place where the bank was maybe two feet above the water. I crouched down in some tall grass and directed my unusually keen vision toward the pool below. The dark green tint of the water told me that it was a deep hole.

See, if you want little fish, you go to shallow water. But if you're stalking four-pounders, you set up shop over a deep hole. This is fairly common knowledge among experienced hunters, but I had to explain it to Drover.

"Now, all we have to do is wait."

"Gosh, that sounds easy!"

"You're catching on, son. You're gonna love this easy life, and just wait until you sink your teeth into that four-pounder."

I was crouched on the bank, my muscles cocked and ready to explode. All I needed was a victim.

The minutes passed. Herds of minnows swam past, little perch, a couple of small bass, water spiders, more minnows, and more minnows. I was about to fall asleep . . .

Then I saw something large. This was no minnow, no measly perch. It was BIG. Every muscle in my highly conditioned body waited for the command to strike.

It was a turtle. "How would you feel about a nice mud turtle for supper, Drover?"

"I don't like mud. Hank, I'm starving."

"Patience, son. Ah ha! Look what's right behind the turtle."

This was it, the one we had been waiting for—a huge, enormous, fat fish.

"There's our fish," I whispered. "Range: six feet. Depth: eighteen inches. Bearing: oh-two-zero-zero. Speed: just about right. Ready. Aim. BONZAI!"

I exploded out of my attack position, reached maximum altitude, leveled off, straightened out, and began my plunge toward the unsuspecting fish. As I streaked toward the water in a graceful arc, the fish appeared even larger than before. Indeed, the thought crossed my mind that Drover and I together wouldn't be able to eat him.

Most experts regard fish as fairly stupid animals, yet we must give them credit for having a certain dull-witted instinct for survival. Even though my attack was perfectly planned and flawlessly executed, somehow the fish got wind of it. And with one flick of his tail, he vanished.

Cancelling the mission at that point was out of the question. I mean, you get into some heavy physics, with thrust and forces and vectors and other stuff that's much too complicated to go into. It's the kind of stuff we deal with every day in the security business but . . .

The point is that once you get a mass of pure muscle traveling downward at a high rate of speed, the physical forces unleashed can't be reversed. Furthermore, in the event that someone miscalculated the depth of the water, this projectile is likely to enter the creek, pass through the shallow liquid, and strike the bottom with tremendous force.

That derned creek wasn't nearly as deep as I thought, never mind what color it was. I buried my nose in six inches of mud on the bottom.

And before you laugh at my misfortune and pass it off as just one of life's many jokes, let me point out just how serious it is when a guy gets his nose buried in six inches of mud— *under the danged water.*

Okay, first of all, your nose doesn't just pop out of the mud, right? And second of all, it's very hard to breathe when you're trapped in deadly quicksand—well, mud. And third of all, stasstisstics, satisticks, suhtickles . . . numbers collected by governmental agencies show that most of the people and animals who drowned between 1945 and 1984 *had their heads under water.*

So laugh if you wish, but this was a life-threatening situation. I could have very easily by George drownded.

No ordinary dog could have gotten out of that pit of deadly quicksand. I mean, that stuff didn't just hold me, it was trying to suck me down, deeper and deeper.

I tried to call for help, but as you might have already surmised, that didn't work. I kicked all four legs in the air. I thrashed, I fought, I twisted and turned and flailed the water, and with each frash and thrail . . . uh, thrash and frail, my life inched closer to darkness and doom.

I repeat: no ordinary dog could have escaped this gruesome death. I escaped. Just follow the logic to its conclusion. When you have logic doing your talking, you don't need to brag.

With only seconds of life left, I tore myself from the clutches of the deadly Quicksand Monster, and before he could get me again, I staggered out onto dry land.

Drover was there, wagging his tail. "Did you catch the fish? How'd you get all that mud on your nose?"

Gasping for breath, I collapsed on the bank. "Never mind . . . the danged fish . . . don't go near . . . that water . . . horrible Quicksand Monster . . . tried to kill me . . . fought him off . . . just barely made it."

Drover rolled his eyes around. "Where'd he go?"

"Water . . . deep, bottomless pit . . . stay back."

"Hank, I want to go home."

42

"No, it's all right . . . whipped him, ran him back into the pit . . . just one thing, Drover."

"What?"

At last I caught my breath. "Under the circumstances, I think it would be a good idea for us to have minnows for supper."

G. L. Holmes

CHAPTER

5

THE LOVELY MISS SCAMPER

We were in the process of moving our
hunting camp downstream to shallow-
er water, when all at once we heard a car coming down the hill toward the crossing. We
waited for it to pass.

It didn't pass, and it wasn't a car. It was an
old green Chevy pickup. It slowed down and
came to a stop in the middle of the low water
crossing.

This struck me as very suspicious. I mean,
darkness was coming on. Why would someone stop a pickup in the middle of the crossing
with darkness coming on?

"Hey, Drover. Lie down flat in this tall grass
and don't make a sound."

"What's the matter?"

"Shhh! Unless I'm badly mistaken, we've just found ourselves a cattle rustler."

"Oh my gosh! I didn't know cattle could drive a pickup."

"What? No, no, you don't understand." I explained about cattle rustlers. "You see, cattle rustling is one of the crimes we're hired to stop. It's part of the job."

He crouched down in the grass. "I thought we didn't have a job. Didn't we quit?"

"Technically speaking, yes. But at a deeper level, Drover, a cowdog can never resign his commission. It's our job to protect the world, not just one ranch. And cattle rustlers are our sworn enemies."

"Are they mean?"

"The very meanest sort of riff-raff. They're hardened crinimals, extremely dangerous."

Drover gulped. "Hank, how far is it to the machine shed?"

"About three miles."

"If a guy got scared out here and wanted to hide, where would he go?"

"He'd just have to stand his ground and fight, Drover, that's the long and short of it. Now shut your little trap and let's watch this thing develop. Memorize every detail."

A man got out of the pickup and stretched. Description: medium height, slim build, age 40, dark narrow eyes, a big drooping black mustache between his nose and upper lip.

Clothing: straw hat, short-sleeved western shirt with snap buttons, black boots with underslung heels, blue jeans, leather belt with "Baxter" on the back.

There was something familiar about this guy. I'd run into him somewhere before, and I was willing to bet that he had a crinimal record as long as your leg.

He walked a couple of steps to his right and looked over into the bed of the pickup, and then he spoke to someone: "How you doing, Scamp? You stay in the back. I won't be long."

I nudged Drover in the ribs. Must have scared him 'cause he squawked. "Shhh! You want to get us shot?"

"No."

"All right, then keep quiet. I just wanted to point out that our suspect is named Baxter."

"How'd you know that?"

"Son, after you've spent years in this business, you remember certain names and faces. That guy's a notorious outlaw. He's been around. And what worries me is that he's got his gang in the back of the pickup."

Drover peeked over the top of the grass. "I don't see anyone."

"Well, silly, do you think they're going to stand up and do handsprings? Of course not. They're hiding back there, which is just another clue that they're up to no good."

"How far did you say it was to the machine shed?"

"Shhhh!"

The notorious Baxter reached into the pickup bed and came out with a . . . what was it? A gun? A knife? I squinted and whispered to Drover, "What is that thing he just pulled out?"

"Looks like a bucket to me."

"A bucket! Don't be absurd. Listen, this guy's a dangerous outlaw. He wouldn't defend himself with a bucket."

"Oh. Okay."

But you know what? It *was* a danged bucket, which just didn't fit the usual M.O. (*Modus of Operationus*). He climbed down the cement crossing, went to the creek, and filled the bucket with water.

"Now, what's that guy up to? Wait, I've got it. He's stealing fish. Yes sir, he's poaching."

"I thought you said he was a cattle ruffler."

"It's *rustler,* and with his record, he's liable to do anything, as long as it's against the law."

"Oh. Well, I hope he has better luck catching fish than you did or we'll be up all night."

"That's very possible, Drover, but if that's what it takes to work this case, that's what we'll do."

The suspect filled his bucket, climbed back to the road, set the bucket down, opened the hood of his pickup, took the cap off the radiator, and started pouring the water.

Drover raised up and stared. "He's putting fish in his motor!"

I studied the evidence and sifted through all

the clues. "You're right, Drover. Somehow this just doesn't fit the pattern. There's something very peculiar going on here."

At that moment, I saw a head appear out of the bed of the pickup—not a human head, as you might have expected, but the head of a dog.

Description: Beagle, age approximately two years three months. Long ears. White band around a nose dotted with brown freckles. Gorgeous big brown eyes just below long lashes.

Summary: The second suspect was not only a woman, but an uncommonly beautiful beagle dog who instantly raised my blood pressure and made me forget that Baxter was putting fish into his radiator.

She looked in our direction and barked. It was a half-bark, half-bay that is common among your fox hounds, your blood hounds, your bassets, and your beagles. She had seen us, and I had no choice but to go up there and ask her a few questions.

"Drover, you stay here and . . ."

He had seen her too. "Hank, that's a woman! And gosh, she's awful cute. I'm going with you."

"All right, but stay behind me and don't get in the way."

We came out of our hiding place and swaggered up to the pickup. "Evening, ma'am. My name's Hank the Cowdog, Head of Ranch Security. I'll need to ask you a few questions."

"My goodness," she said in a sultry voice, "look what's come out of the shadows! They call me Miss Scamper."

"And I'm Drover!"

"Shut up, Drover. Miss Scamper, sagebrush is purple and cactus is green, you're the prettiest beagle that I've ever seen."

She grinned. "My, my, you go right to the truth of the matter, don't you."

Drover couldn't keep his yap shut. "Fence posts are brown and barbed wire is rusted, the first time I saw you my heart pret' near busted."

"Shut up, Drover."

Miss Scamper fluttered them long eyelashes. "You boys are just full of yourselves tonight."

I gave Drover an elbow and tried to push him under the pickup. "Yes ma'am, but I should warn you about Drover. He's very mealy-mouthed and insincere, but speaking for myself, I'd have to say that the most beautiful sunset in the world is just a flashlight compared to you.''

''You could be right about that, big boy. Did you say you had some questions to ask me?''

''Yeah!'' Up popped Drover again. ''Will you be my girlfriend?''

''Get lost, Drover.'' I kicked him out of the way. ''Yes ma'am, I've got a question or two. Where do you stay?''

''Well now, I don't ordinarily give out that information.'' She gave me a wink. ''But to the Head of Ranch Security, my goodness, I just about have to tell, don't I?''

''Uh, yes ma'am, I'd say it's your civic duty.''

''Yeah-yus indeed, and I'm a very civic woman.''

For a moment there, I stopped breathing. ''Yes ma'am, you're about as civic as any woman I ever laid eyes on.''

''I'm so glad you're in the security business,'' she fluffed at her hair, ''or I might be feeling . . . ah . . . insecure.'' She wiggled her eyebrows.

''Yes ma'am, but I can assure you that your safret will be seek with me . . . uh, your secret will be safe with me.''

''I'll bet,'' she said, almost in a whisper.

G.L.Holmes

"Next ranch down the creek. Make a left at the mailbox. I'm there most of the time."

"I see. Well, uh, do you have a big fightin' boyfriend?"

"None that should bother you, big boy. I always enjoy cultivating new friends."

Drover crawled between my legs. "I'll be your friend!"

I shoved him away. "Well, I can already see that this case is going to require some serious investigation, Miss Scamper, and I think what I'd better do is take a little ride in the moonlight with you."

"Whatever the law requires, big boy." I sprang up into the back of the pickup and sat down beside her. She looked me up and down. "Oooo! You're quite a jumper, aren't you?"

"I'm saving my best tricks for later, ma'am"

"I'll bet."

Drover tried to get in, but couldn't quite make it. "Hank, I want to go too. Don't leave me!"

"You stay here and scout the fish situation. I'll be back in a couple of days." I looked at Miss Scamper. "Or weeks."

The hood slammed. Baxter came around and set the bucket into the back. Now I remembered where I'd seen him. He'd helped Slim and Loper at the fall branding last year.

Anyone could have mistaken . . . even though he was one of our neighbors on the creek, he *looked* very much like a cattle rustler and . . . never mind.

He glared at me, and I gave him a big friendly grin, as if to say, "Hi there, how's it going?"

"What do you think you're doing, pooch?"

Before I could answer, he grabbed me by the scruff of the neck and one back leg and pitched me into the creek. When I came up for air, I saw the pickup pulling away.

And Miss Scamper was waving goodbye.

CHAPTER
6

UNEXPECTED COMPANY

There for a minute I was afraid the Quick-sand Monster was going to get me again, but I swam to shore with extra strong strokes and managed to escape.

I climbed out on the bank and shook myself. Drover stood nearby, looking his usual simple self.

"Hank, did you jump or did that man throw you out?"

"What do you think?"

"Well . . . I wasn't sure, and I thought I'd ask."

"He threw me out, you dunce, and it's all your fault. If it hadn't been for you, I'd be taking a moonlight ride with a beautiful beagle right this minute. I hope you're happy."

Drover sneezed. "Well, I am kind of happy.

I didn't want to stay here by myself 'cause . . ." He rolled his eyes and looked up in the big cottonwood trees that grew along the bank. "Hank, it's getting dark and I'm scared and I'm hungry and I want to go home."

"Well, that's tough. We quit our jobs so we could go on the road and find romance, and we ain't going back until we do. In fact, we ain't going back period."

He started sniffling. "But Hank, you promised I could go back home after we lived off the land."

"No, no. If you'll recall my exact words, I promised I'd take it under advisement. I've taken it under advisement and the answer is forget it. Come on, let's move on down the creek. Stay behind me and I don't want to hear any more yapping and whimpering out of you."

I found a cow trail on the east bank and followed it in a northeasterly direction. I checked the stars and did a few navigational complications . . . commutations . . . what is the danged word? Computations.

I did my navigation stuff, but even more important, I knew that if we followed this creek far enough, we'd end up on the ranch where

Beulah stayed. Ah, sweet Beulah! The mere thought of that fair lady made me see stars that weren't in the sky.

Well, I was padding along, lost in delicious thoughts of my one and only true love, when Drover cranked up his Mister Pitiful routine again.

"Hank!"

"Hush, Drover."

"But Hank!"

"I said hush, and in my line of work, hush means hush."

"But Hank . . . behind you!"

"Of course you're behind me. You were behind me the day you were born, and everything you've done since then has merely confirmed . . ."

"Hank, we're in trouble!"

I stopped. Drover ran into me. It was very dark by this time, no moon at all because we were beneath big cottonwoods that blocked out the moonlight.

I poked him in the chest. "Now listen, you sawed-off, stub-tailed, feather-brained little squeak box. I imposed a ban on talking, and for a very good reason. This is coyote country, son, and I don't think it would be real smart to advertise our location. In case you don't know it, them guys are basically stupid but very dangerous."

Would you believe it? The runt *growled* at me. Hey, I'll take a growl or two off some dogs, but not off Drover. I mean, a very important part of heading up the Security Division lies in knowing how to control and motivate your employees, don't you see. You give 'em just enough slack so they can do their job, but every now and then you have to yank 'em back in line.

On my outfit, insubordination is not allowed, and growling at the Boss is insubordination.

I gave him a pop on the nose, just to get his attention. "Now shut your trap and let's move out."

We moved out, through bushes and grapevines, over rocks and fallen logs. Drover was sure making a lot of noise back there. Sounded like there were four of us on the trail instead of two.

"Holy cats, Drover, pick up your feet!"

"Hank!"

"Hush, silence!"

I had been aware for a long time that Drover lacked, shall we say, grace and agility. To put it bluntly, he was clumsy. I mean, he lacked the physical gifts you look for in a sure-nuff, top-of-the-line cowdog. I had learned to put up with his short-comings, but I'd never learned to like 'em.

Well, there we were on a "silent" march through coyote country, and he sounded like a cow on snowshoes. "Drover, if you don't pick up your feet and quit running into bushes . . . wait a minute, halt, hold it right here."

We came to a stop. I sniffed the air. "I'm getting a reading on a peculiar smell. You picked it up yet?"

"Yes."

"I've smelled it before, I'm sure I have. What do you reckon it is?"

"Could it be . . . coyotes?"

I sniffed again. "Not likely. They'd have to be very close for us to get that strong a reading, and there's no way they could have slipped up on us while I was in the scout position. Don't forget who's in charge around here."

"Okay. But Hank . . ."

"Let's move . . ." There was just enough moonlight filtering through the trees so that I could see a little bit of Drover's head. "What's happened to your nose?"

"What?"

"Your nose. Looks like it got caught in a pencil sharpener. Has it always been that long and sharp?"

"No."

"Then how do you explain . . . hey, your eyes weren't yellow this morning, were they?"

"No."

"Something's haywire here. You've undergone a complete transformation. You don't look yourself any more. If I didn't know better, I'd say you were a . . . HUH?"

There was a moment of silence, then Drover's voice: "A coyote, Hank?"

"Right. Let me ask you one more question, Drover. Are we in T-R-O-U-B-L-E?"

"Y-E-S."

I gulped and cleared my throat. I spoke to the mysterious head with the long nose and the yellow eyes. "Good evening. My name is Hank the Cowdog. Uh, my friend and I were out on a walk, soaking up the sounds and smells of the night, you might say, and uh we hadn't expected company, but it uh appears that you've joined us. May I ask to whom I'm speaking?"

"You talking Rip and Snort," came the reply in a deep voice.

"Rip and Snort! Well I'll be dadburned,

what a coincidence. We were just looking for you guys."

"Hunk not smart to look for Rip and Snort. Many time Hunk make Rip and Snort look foolish. Coyote not like that, get mad, fighting and tearing up everything. Now we capture. Hunk in large trouble, not get away this time."

"Get away? Captured? Hey listen, we've been looking for you guys for over an hour."

"Uh. How come you look?"

I leaned over and whispered in his ear. "Snort, you remember the night me and you and your brother went over to that old silage pit?" He grunted. I guess that meant yes. "Didn't we have a blast that night?"

"What means, 'blast'? It means like boom-boom?"

In the coyote dialect, "boom-boom" means gun, so as you can see, we had a little problem with the translation. It was a lucky thing that I was fluent in many languages.

"No, what I'm saying is that we had a great time. You remember?"

"Um."

"We ate that silage, got a little plastered, went up on that hill, and sang all night long?"

There was just enough moonlight for me to detect a drooling effect in Snort's mouth. In other words, the mere mention of drinking and carousing had made his mouth water.

This was all part of my plan, don't you see, and it was beginning to work.

"And Snort, the reason we were looking for you tonight is that I kind of forgot how to get over to that silage pit. Now, I'm sure you're too busy to go with us, but maybe you could give me directions."

"Me talk with brother."

For several minutes they mumbled and muttered. I had nothing to do but count my heartbeats (three hundred and twenty-seven) and wait. I didn't hear a peep out of Drover.

They finished their conference and Snort spoke. "Brother not want take Hunk and little white dog. Brother hungry, want EAT Hunk and little white dog, then go sing and drinking. What Hunk say about that?"

"Well, uh . . ." I was thinking fast. ". . . as you might expect, guys, I think that's not a real good plan. In the first place, dog meat's not all that good—they tell me, I haven't tried it myself. In the second place, if you guys took the time to eat two whole dogs, you'd be so full and sleepy, you'd never make it to the silage pit.

"And last but not least, we have the matter of friendship and brotherhood. You guys can't expect to keep friends if you go around eating them. Oh, and one more thing. You'll need a tenor for the singing. So I think you'll agree . . ."

Snort grunted. "We talk. Hunk not leave."

"Me leave? Why I wouldn't think of it."

As a matter of fact, that was a small lie. I'd thought about it a bunch. The major problem in trying to make a run for it was that those two thugs had excellent noses. They could have tracked down a sugar ant in a four section pasture, in the dead of the night.

They mumbled and muttered some more. Then Snort turned back to me with the verdict. "We go silage pit, drink, have fun oh boy, sing many coyote song."

"Hey, that sounds great, Snort."

"Then we think about eat dog."

"Uh . . . I still say that eating your friends is bad manners."

He poked me in the chest with his paw. "Snort not want dog opinion. And Hunk not try escape."

"Who me?"

"Or we have early supper and sing without tenor."

"We don't want that, do we?"

"Make line. Snort in front, Rip behind. Two dogs in middle."

"Yes sir." I took my place in the middle and looked around for little Drover. You know what? The runt had disappeared. Those coyotes had been so busy threatening me, they hadn't even noticed.

They held another conference and discussed whether or not they wanted to take the time to hunt him down, which they most certainly could have done. But they had drinking on their minds and decided to forget about Drover.

As Snort said, sticking his grinning snout right in my face, "Hunk make plenty grub. Save little dog for snack."

So we formed a line and off we went to the silage pit. I was determined to have a good time, since this might be my last opportunity.

ROTTEN MEAT

The silage pit wasn't too far, just a couple of hills west of us. We started off at a walk, but by the time we got up into those caliche hills west of the creek, Snort had picked up the pace.

Up on top, the air was clean and cool, heavy with the smell of new grass and wildflowers. We were out of the trees by then and our path was lighted by a nice fat moon.

Not a bad night for a walk, in other words, unless you happened to be traveling with cannibals. I was kind of sorry Drover wasn't there to enjoy it, the little dunce, how do you reckon he managed to slip away and leave me . . .

Every once in a while he pulls a stunt that makes you wonder just how dumb he really is.

Anyway, the farther we went, the more excited those coyote brothers became. They yipped and howled, skipped and snorted and hopped and laughed. Oh, they were having a big time.

About halfway there, they couldn't hold back any longer and cranked up their Coyote National Anthem and Sacred Hymn:

Me just a worthless coyote, me howling at
the moon,
Me like to sing and holler, me crazy as a
loon.
Me not want job or duties, no church or
Sunday school,
Me just a worthless coyote and me ain't
nobody's fool!

I joined in the singing, though I'd have to say that my heart wasn't in it. I was still studying on how to get out of this mess. It appeared to me that my only hope lay in getting Rip and Snort so drunk on silage that they couldn't walk.

Silage, you might know, is fermented feed stalks. In the late summer, the cowboys run a chopper through a field of corn or cane and dump the chopped stuff into a big pit. They leave it sit there for six months or a year and then feed it to the cattle.

If you're a cow, you like to eat it in the wintertime. If you're a lazy, shiftless coyote, you like to drink the squeezings just any time of the day or night, in the winter, spring, summer, or fall. It contains alkyhall, don't you see.

When we got within a hundred yards of the pit, Snort couldn't stand the suspense any longer, and he broke into a dead gallop. I hoped his brother would do the same, but he didn't. He stayed behind me, nudging me along with his sharp nose, and I had no chance to escape.

When me and Rip got inside the pit, we found old Snort right in the middle of it. His mouth was crammed with silage. He'd chew a while and spit hulls a while, then gobble some more. Rip piled in beside him and started eating his way into the silage.

I stood back and watched. This was part of my strategy, see, to let them boys make pigs of themselves and then I'd skip out. Worked fine for the first hour. Just as they were starting to weave and get silly, Snort noticed me. Maybe he saw a sly glint in my eyes.

He ordered me into the silage. I want to make that very clear. He *forced* it on me.

"Okay," I said to myself, "I'll take a few

bites, just to keep up appearances.'' So I took a couple of bites. And another couple of bites. And a few more, just for show, and . . .

An yew no what? That shilage ish pretty good shtuff, once shyou get ushed to the bitter tashte.

What I'm building up to is that one thing led to another. I sort of got involved in the festivities and forgot I was amongst savages. I forgot all about their plans for supper, but even better, *they did too.*

I have hazy memories of much of the night, but I do recall that the sun came up in the east, which meant that it was morning. By this time Rip and Snort and I had become the very best of friends.

Snort suggested that we go back down to the creek and take a cold bath, so we staggered out of the pit and weaved our way in that direction. Good thing the creek was located at the bottom of a hill. I'm not sure we could have found it anywhere else.

Well, we were making our way across a grassy flat, heading for the creek, when all of a sudden Snort's nose flew up in the air and he came to a stop.

''Ha! Smell something berry good to eat!''

Rip's nose went up and so did mine. I gave

the air a good sniffing. "That's funny, Snort, all I smell is a skunk."

His yellow eyes sparkled. At the time I didn't know what that meant. He took off in a kind of sideways lope, and me and Rip came along behind.

I wasn't sure what we were doing until I glanced up ahead and saw two big black birds standing in the middle of a feed trail. They appeared to be eating breakfast. I had a suspicion that they were a couple of buzzards named Wallace and Junior, and I had a pretty good idea what they were eating.

YUCK!!

Snort took dead aim at the buzzards and picked up speed. He was on a collision course.

Old man Wallace heard us coming. His ugly bald head shot up and he glared at us. "Hyah! Y'all get on outa here, don't you dare touch our breakfast, we got here first, Junior, don't you let them, you fight 'em off, son, while I . . ."

Snort lit right in the middle of them, and you talk about feathers flying! I don't think Junior ever knew what hit him, but the old man sure did, and he must have lost a bushel of feathers flapping his wings and trying to get airborne.

He taxied into the wind and finally got himself off the ground, just as Snort made a dive at him and bit off half his tail.

Junior got knocked over backwards, did a couple of back flips, and came up sitting down. "Oh g-g-gosh, P-Pa, there's a w-w-wolf!"

Old man Wallace flew in a wide circle and landed in a cottonwood tree nearby. Snort

G.L. Holmes

came back to the skunk and showed Junior some fangs.

That was enough for Junior. He scrambled to his feet and took cover behind the cottonwood. "W-w-w-wolf, w-wolf, h-h-help, mu-mu-mu-murder!"

By this time, the old man was safe on his perch. "Junior, you git yourself out from behind this tree and go out there and fight for our rights!"

"B-b-b-but P-Pa, it's a w-w-wolf and th-th-they b-b-bite, bite."

"That's no excuse, son. We had that skunk first and he's our property. Now you git out there and quit acting like a danged kid, you hear me?"

"N-n-n-no. I d-don't uh hear a th-th-thing." Junior wasn't kidding. He really couldn't hear—because he had covered both ears with his wings.

"Junior! You git yourself . . ."

"L-l-louder, P-Pa, I c-can't hear y-you."

"Junior! You uncover your ears this very minute or I'm gonna come down . . . danged ungrateful, irresponsible kid!"

"W-what did you s-s-say, P-p-pa?"

"I said, you hush up! And y'all," he turned to us and beamed us an evil glare, "y'all just better git on outa here and leave our breakfast alone, or I'm liable to lose my temper!''

Snort was sitting beside the skunk by this time. He grinned up at old man Wallace. Maybe he was remembering the night over in the canyons when Wallace had, shall we say, upchucked on him and Rip. That's what buzzards do when they get mad, don't you know, but this time Wallace was out of range, and Snort knew it.

He grinned and old Wallace fumed and squawked. Then Snort turned to me and Rip and motioned us over. I wasn't really looking forward to this. Dead skunk has never been one of my favorite foods.

"Now we sing special coyote song," said Snort. "Hunk sing tenor."

So the three of us got together, me in the middle. Snort gave us the pitch (that was pretty funny, Snort trying to find a pitch), gave us three beats. He couldn't count to three, so he counted, "One, four, seven!" And we belted out an old coyote favorite called "Rotten Meat." Snort sang the verses and me and Rip came in on the chorus. Here's how it went.

There's many a mystery's got lost in our
  history

But none more important for us to
  repeat
Than this secret potion, this coyote love
  lotion,
The wonderful essence of ripe stinking
  meat.

Oh, rotten meat, rotten meat!
The odor's deliciously subtle and sweet.
Coyotes love to cheat and we love to
  eat,
This life would be rotten without rotten
  meat.

I know a feller, his coat is dark yeller.
He's got sinus drainage and sneezes a
  lot.
He had no success in the wimmen
  department
Until he discovered the perfume of rot.

Rotten meat, hey, rotten meat!
The odor's deliciously subtle and sweet.
Coyotes love to cheat and we love to
  eat.
This life would be rotten without rotten
  meat.

At this point, Snort turned to me and said, "Now Hunk do verse."

"Well, I don't know. I guess I could try. Let's see here."

The girl of my dreams is a wonderful
  lady.
Miss Beulah's her name and she makes
  my heart thump.
It never occurred to me she might prefer
  me
If I showed up smelling of decomposed
  skunk.

Roll in rotten meat, bathe in rotten
  meat!
The odor's deliciously subtle and sweet.
Coyotes love to cheat and we love to
  eat,
This life would be rotten without rotten
  meat.

Snort took the last verse.

The secret of courtship in coyote circles
Depends on the deep manly smell of the
  guy.

A woman worth courting wants guys
who are sporting,
Who stink to high heaven and smell to
the sky!

We wear rotten meat, we share rotten
meat!
The aftershave lotion that's sure hard to
beat.
Coyotes always smell neat, we've ac-
complished the feat
Of charming our wimmen with rotten
meat!

Well, we harmonized on that last chord and
it was just by George beautiful. But to no one's
surprise, old man Wallace had something
smart to say.

"Huh! That's the worst singing I've heard
since that last time you hammerheads got
together."

"Oh yeah?" I called back. "When we need
an authority on music and culture, we won't
ask the opinion of a buzzard."

"You could do worse, son. In fact, you just
did."

I ignored him. I mean, any time you try to

do something daring in the field of culture, you're going to have small minds finding fault. Greatness has always been a lonely profession.

I turned to Snort. "Guys, that was a wonderful job."

"Ha! Hunk do good too, make pretty good coyote."

"Yeah, well, I've got a few talents tucked away. But let me ask you something. You really believe that stuff about women flipping over the smell of rotten meat?"

He nodded. "Berry strong medicine, work many time, never fail."

"Hm. I knew they went wild over the smell of sewer water, but I've never tried rolling in rotten meat. You think it might work on this gal of mine?"

Rip moved over and whispered something in his brother's ear. Then Snort said, "Brother say rotten smell work on dog woman for sure, but not if coyote brothers decide eat Hunk for breakfast."

"Well I . . . yes, I see what you mean, but uh, I thought we had sort of . . . that is, I thought our relationship had, well, become more meaningful that that."

They stared at me with drunken yellow eyes and shook their heads. "Maybe so, maybe not.

First we roll on skunk, have big coyote feast. Then we talk.''

I was still in trouble, fellers, and my life was hanging by a thread. You can find a needle in a haystack, but thread comes on a spool.

CHAPTER

8

NOT JUST ONE BRILLIANT MANEUVER, BUT SEVERAL

For all I knew, this would be my last meal on earth—also my first and last roll on a dead skunk. I decided what the heck, I might as well try to enjoy it.

Rip and Snort went first. I watched and took a few mental notes. First they got down on their bellies and crawled around on the skunk. Then they flipped over on their backs and wiggled around and kicked all four legs in the air. Then they hopped up and gave themselves a big shake.

Well, that looked easy enough. I dived in, rolled, kicked, did the whole routine. After I had shooked myself, I turned to Snort. "Well, what do you think? Did I do it right?"

"Pretty good. Now we have big coyote feast, oh boy!"

I glanced down at the dead skunk. You might recall that on one of my previous adventures, I sat in on a big coyote feast where "aged mutton" was on the menu. It didn't do much for me. Well, yes it did. It made me sick, and I mean SICK. "Tell you what, fellers, I'm not real hungry right this minute, and maybe I'll pass on the grub."

Snort gave me an unfriendly glare. "You want make coyote angry?"

"Angry? Why, heavens no."

"You want insult coyote hospitality? Berry bad manners turning down coyote feast."

"Well I . . ."

"And when coyote get mad, want fresh meat—maybeso dog meat." The two savages stared at me. I noticed that Rip licked his chops, and I thought I detected a hungry glimmer in his eyes.

I coughed. "I see what you mean. No, I think you misunderstood. What I meant to say was that I'll go first, and I wondered if you guys would be upset if I ate the whole skunk myself. After all, I'm your guest."

They went into a huddle and discussed it in

whispers. Then Snort turned back to me. "That not work. Hunk not eat first."

"Now hold on. The guest always eats first and gets first dibs on the grub. That's only fair and decent."

Snort shook his head. "Coyote not give hoot for fair and decent. Coyote tradition say guest eat *last*."

"Well, that's an outrage! Do you expect me to take that kind of treatment?" Their heads bobbed up and down. "Very well, we'll eat in the coyote tradition, but I'll have to demand a fair and equal division of the meat."

Snort pushed himself up and swaggered over to me and stuck his sharp nose right in my face. "Coyote not like demand and not give hoot for equal division."

"I'm sorry, Snort, but fair is fair and right is right. I want my equal share of the skunk. Otherwise, there's nothing to keep you guys from hogging the whole thing."

Snort started laughing, then Rip joined in. They had a good chuckle. "Ha! At last Hunk understand coyote manners."

"What are you saying? Surely you don't mean . . ."

He poked me with his paw. "In coyote tradition, coyote eat and guest *watch*."

"Now wait just a minute! If you think I'm going to sit still while you guys . . ." He lifted his lips and displayed his teeth, which were long and sharp. And he also growled. "All right, calf-rope, I surrender. Just this once we'll eat in the coyote tradition."

"Hunk pretty smart dog."

"You got that right, Charlie," I muttered.

"Huh?"

"I said, thanks."

Snort gave a yip and a howl and dived into the middle of the skunk. Rip did the same, and within seconds they were in the midst of a terrible fight. They snapped and they snarled and they slugged and they gouged. Brotherhood among the cannibals can be a pretty rough affair. Nobody but a coyote could survive it.

Well, they rolled off the skunk, don't you see, and all of a sudden Junior's head appeared around the edge of the cottonwood tree. He looked left and right and hopped over to the skunk. He snatched it up in his beak and hustled back behind the tree.

Upstairs on his perch, old man Wallace watched the whole thing. When he saw Junior steal the skunk, he brought his right wing to rest over his heart.

"Oh son, my boy! All these many years I've

G.L. Holmes

waited for a sign, and there it is, right before my very eyes! Praise the Lord, the boy's gonna make something of himself, save me a leg, son, I'll be right down!''

He stepped off the limb, spread his wings, and crash-landed in a plum thicket.

Rip and Snort missed the whole thing, didn't see any of it. They were still trying to tear each other apart, rolling around and chewing on

each other. The air was filled with dust and coyote hair.

Next thing I knew, I heard a yip-yip-yip off to my left, followed by a big deep roof-roof-roof! I looked around and guess what I saw: Mister Half-Stepper came flying across the creek, and right behind him, in hot and deadly pursuit, was an old enemy of mine, Rufus the Doberman Pinscher.

And Drover was not half-stepping. He was showing a kind of speed I'd never seen before, never mind his bad leg and allergies.

He came streaking right up to me. "Oh Hank, help, murder, mayday, mayday, he's going to kill me, what am I going to do!!"

That was an interesting question, and quite frankly, I didn't have an answer worked out by the time he slid to a stop and took cover behind me. An even more interesting question was, *what was I going to do*?

I had a suspicion that after Rufus tore Drover to shreds, he'd get a kick out of shredding me too. And he, being a ferocious doberman pinscher, was just the guy who could do it.

"Drover, I'd rather you didn't take cover behind me. Rufus is liable to think we're friends."

"But Hank, I think he wants to fight!"

"What ever gave you that idea? Just because his little green eyes are flaming and he's got slobber dripping off his fangs?"

"Yeah, and he said so too."

"Well, this is your fight, son. I'm just a neutral party."

"But Hank!"

Rufus came stalking up, the muscles rippling up his long thin legs and into this shoulders. He had his pointed ears down in fighting position, and his evil eyes were blazing.

Kind of scared me, if you want to know the truth.

"Morning, Rufus. What brings you out on a . . ."

"Shaddap, cowdog. Let me have him. I'm gonna tear him apart."

"Don't let him, Hank! Remember, I'm just a chicken-hearted little mutt, and my leg hurts."

"Hey look, Rufus, he didn't mean any harm."

"He was trespassing on my ranch. Get out of

my way or I'll trespass you."

"Would you actually do a thing like that?"

He gave me a snarling grin. "In a New York minute. Just give me a reason."

"Will this be a fair fight between you and Drover?"

"As fair as it needs to be, cowdog."

Drover started moaning. "No Hank, don't let him hurt me!"

"Drover, you got into this mess by yourself and you'll have to get out of it by yourself. It ain't my fight."

"Now you're talking sense," said Rufus. "You just run along and keep out of my way and you won't get hurt."

"Thanks, Rufus, I worry about getting hurt."

"Oh Hank," Drover cried, "I never thought I'd hear you say that! I thought you were fearless and brave."

"Most of the time I am, Drover, but I try to stay out of the way of doberman pinschers."

Rufus liked that. "You may be smarter than you look, cowdog. Let's get the fight started. I got things to do."

"Oh Hank!"

"All right, let's get it started," I said. "But

first, I'd like for you to meet a couple of pals of mine."

"I ain't interested in your pals."

"I understand that, but you're going to be fighting on their property and I think it would be a good idea . . . I'm sure you understand."

"All right," he growled, "but make it quick."

"It won't take but a minute. Come on." The three of us walked over to the spot where Rip and Snort were tearing up the grass and gouging holes in the earth. "Hey, Snort, hold up a second." They kept fighting. "Hey! Back off and shut up, I've got an important message for you."

The snarling stopped. Rip and Snort looked at me with puzzled expressions. "Not good you butt into family discussion."

"I know Snort, but this is important. Rufus here has something he wants to tell you." All eyes swung to Rufus. "Go ahead and tell 'em what you told me, Rufus."

His little eyes went from me to the coyotes and back to me. "Say, what is this!"

"All right, I'll tell 'em. Snort, Rufus just ate your whole skunk and he wanted you to know that it was real good." Two pairs of coyote eyes swept the spot where the skunk had been. "And he also wondered if that was grounds for a fight, because if it is, he said you boys better go get four or five of your coyote pals to make it a fair fight."

The brothers stood up, and so did the hair on their backs. "Not like smart-mouth dog! Not like skunk all gone!"

"Hey listen . . ."

"And Rufus said if you boys know what's good for you, you'll tuck your tails and head for the house."

Low rumbling sounds started coming from the throats of the coyote brothers. Snort stepped toward Rufus. "Rip and Snort not need help for fight!"

"You dope, can't you see what he's doing?" said Rufus.

"Snort, he called you a dope."

Rufus turned to me. "Why you low-down, sewer-dipping, pot-licking, double-cross-ing . . ."

"Are you going to take that, Snort? Just give me the word and we'll teach him a lesson."

Snort didn't give any word. But what he lacked in language skills he made up for in sheer meanness. He and his brother pinned back their ears and moved in for battle.

Rufus started backing up. "Stupid, that's what you are, a couple of stupid stinking coyotes! Can't you see what he's doing? Hey listen, we can get together on this . . ."

They got together, all right, Rufus on the bottom, Snort in the middle, and Rip up on top. The wreck was on, fellers, and me and Drover had to step back to keep from getting maimed.

It wasn't a bad match, let me tell you. Rufe put up a good tussle and got in some pretty good licks. But of course the terrible thing about fighting those coyote brothers was that the harder the fight and the longer it lasted, the more they loved it.

After a bit Rufe managed to kick them away. That gave him just enough time to gather up those long doberman legs and head for the back side of the pasture. He lit a shuck and headed north, with Rip and Snort right on his sawed-off tail.

"Well, Drover, we've solved another case and it's time to move along. I believe my true love is waiting."

CHAPTER
9

THE CASE OF
THE MYSTERIOUS
DEAD HORSE

We went padding down the creek, enjoy-
ing the scenery and the freshness of
morning. It was a beautiful day, but what made
it even more beautiful was that my thoughts
had turned to the lovely maiden, Miss Beulah
of the long collie nose and the fair flaxen hair.

I wondered if she'd been thinking about me.
I had little doubt that she had been, for she was
a smart lady and had excellent taste.

Yet it was hard to explain her strange attach-
ment to Plato the Bird Dog. In some ways Plato was a likeable mutt. He had no glaring flaws
but also no glaring virtues. He was the kind of
guy you might choose as a casual friend, but

certainly not worthy of the love of a refined collie.

I mean, just consider what kind of dog would go around chasing birds. Compare that to, well, me for instance. I chased *monsters,* not birds. I fought coons and badgers and coyotes and poisonous snakes.

I had a glamorous job, enormous responsibility, and the dashing good looks you expect in a blue-ribbon, top-of-the-line cowdog. I also had better than average gifts as a poet, philosopher, and singer.

When you add that all up, what you get is by George overwhelming evidence that Beulah never should have given a second glance to Plato. But she had. Why? It just didn't make any sense.

But I knew one thing for sure: Plato was in for some hard times. I had nothing personal against the mutt, but he was fixing to lose himself a girlfriend.

"Boy, you sure fixed old Rufus."

"Huh?" It was Drover speaking. "Oh. You liked that?"

"Gosh yes! There for a minute, I thought you'd forgotten our friendship."

"I've tried to forget it, Drover, but somehow it just hasn't worked out."

"Thanks, Hank. It means a lot to hear you say that. I guess you saved my life."

"Yup."

"I don't know what I can do to pay you back."

"May I make a suggestion?"

"Sure Hank, anything at all."

"When we get over on the next ranch, I'm going to be doing some serious courting. It would please me enormously if you would try not to embarrass me with childish remarks and stupid behavior."

"Sure, Hank. That'll be easy, 'cause I'm going to be courting too."

"Oh? And whom will you be courting, if I may ask?"

"Why, Beulah, of course."

"Halt! Hold it right here." I put my nose right down in the runt's face. "No you *won't* be courting Beulah, because *I'm* going to be courting Beulah."

His simple smile wilted. "Oh gosh. You mean we're in love with the same girl?"

"No. I'm in love with the same girl and you're having wild delusions. What you must remember, Drover, is that your emotions are shallow, immature, and based on false expectations. I hate to put it this way, but you're just not in Beulah's class."

"But Hank, the last time I was around her, I kind of got the feeling that maybe she was a little bit sweet on me."

"No. She was being nice to you. She didn't want to hurt your feelings. She didn't want to come right out and club you over the head with the truth—that she was madly, hopelessly in love with me."

"Oh."

"And possibly with Plato, to a small degree."

"Oh."

"I'm sorry."

"Drat."

"There's no easy way to say it."

"Well, it may hurt for a while, but it sure doesn't feel good."

"Exactly, but you see, what you're feeling is mere puppy love, not the deeper, more refined emotions described throughout the ages by poets and troubadours."

"Oh shucks. Well, if you've got a case of puppy love, what do you do about it?"

I gave that some thought. "Suffer, I think. Suffer quietly. But that's not so bad, Drover, because it's a well known fact that suffering builds character."

"No fooling?"

"That's right. As odd as it may sound, the more you suffer, the stronger you become."

"So if I suffer for a couple of hours, maybe I'll be ready for Beulah?"

"Uh . . . no. These things take weeks, sometimes months. Your assignment is to suffer quietly, build up your character, stay out of my way, and basically shut up. Can you handle that?"

"Well," he scratched his ear, "if I can remember all of that. Let's see: The suffering you are, the character it hurts. Did I get it right?"

"Close enough, Drover. We can't expect perfection the first day. Come on, let's make tracks. There's a certain woman down the creek who's waiting for her life to begin."

We followed the creek for another half-mile or so, until we came to the water gap. We slithered under the bottom wire and came out on Beulah's ranch.

"Hold it right here," I said. "Take a deep breath, Drover. Don't you think the air smells sweeter and more excruciating over here?"

Drover put his nose up in the air and filled

his lungs. Then he started coughing. "Oh my gosh, Hank, something's dead around here!"

"What?" I tested the wind and smelled nothing. "You must be mistaken, Drover. I'm not picking up a thing."

"You can't smell *that*? It must be a dead horse. It's awful!"

"Hmm. All right, we'll mark this spot with an X and start walking in opposite directions, making a large circle. This may turn out to be something routine, or . . . it could be the first clue in the Case of the Dead Horse. Let's move out, and call out your readings every now and then."

We put our tails together over the X, and on my command, we began marching in opposite directions. Funny, I still wasn't getting a reading on my smellometer, but every now and then I would hear Drover call out, "It's getting weaker!"

I couldn't ignore the possibility that Drover was getting a false reading because of his sinus problem, but in this business you have to follow up every lead—even the ones Drover comes up with.

Each of us walked out a semi-circle, and before long we were moving toward each other. I was still drawing a blank, but Drover began picking up signals again. "It's getting stronger, Hank. Stronger. Stronger. Pew!"

We met and I marked another X in the ground. "All right, Drover, we've established the two points of discombobulation. We'll call this X Point Baker and the other one Point Abel."

"Okay."

"We'll draw an imaginary line of intersection between the two points."

"Okay."

"And we'll concentrate our search between Point Abel and Point Baker. I have a feeling that this is going to lead to a very surprising discovery. We could have a murder on our hands."

"Oh my gosh!"

"Now, if my calculations are correct, all we have to do is find the mid-point between the two X's, and there, Drover, we will find the murder victim. Let's go."

We moved out in a straight line, running our sensory equipment at full capacity and checking behind every weed and bush. When we reached the mid-point, I called a halt.

"This is it, Drover," I whispered. "Are you still getting the signals?"

"Gosh yes! But Hank . . ." He rolled his eyes around. "I think it's a dead skunk."

"Ah ha! Now we're getting somewhere. I had my doubts about that dead horse business all along. It just didn't fit. Now listen very carefully to your instructions. Close your eyes and turn your head in a full circle."

"I don't think it'll go in a full circle, Hank. It starts hanging up about halfway around."

"Then turn your entire body, just whatever works. When you get the strongest reading, stop and hold your position. Ready? Go."

He closed his eyes and started turning in a circle. "Hank, I'm getting dizzy."

"Tough it out, son. There could be a promotion in this thing if you can crack the case."

"Okay, I'll do my best."

"Your best is the very least you can do, Drover."

He turned in a full circle and stopped. "There it is, Hank! It's right here in front of my nose!"

"You're pointing at *me,* you dunce. Somehow you've managed to bungle another . . ." Suddenly the pieces of the puzzle began fitting together. "Wait a minute. Did you say you were picking up dead skunk signals?"

"Yeah. That's got to be what it is, Hank, because nothing smells deader or skunkier than a dead skunk."

"Okay, relax. I've got it worked out." I told him about how Rip and Snort and I had rolled on the skunk. "So once again, you've wasted our valuable time and made a mockery of serious detective work. "

"Well . . ."

"Dead horse!"

"Well . . ."

"The trouble with you, Drover, is that you're wrong only 95% of the time. If you were more consistent, I could ignore everything you say."

"Okay, Hank, but I . . ."

"As it is, I get duped every now and then, and the result is always the same: You end up making a fool of yourself. I'm telling you this for your own good."

"I appreciate it, Hank."

"Come on, let's move on to the romance department."

"Are you going to bathe first? You don't smell too good."

I closed my eyes and shook my head. "Drover, you have missed the entire point. The fragrance of dead skunk is an ancient love potion, known only to tribes of wild coyotes."

"I sure didn't know that."

"Nobody expected you to, son. What you don't know about women would fill several large holes."

He looked up at the clouds. "Sure glad you're not courting me."

"That makes two of us, Drover."

CHAPTER

10

THE PERFUME FLUNKS OUT, BUT ALL IS NOT LOST

We traveled in silence, following the creek past those high bluffs just east of the water gap, around the big horseshoe bend, and through a place where the bottom had grown up in willows and small cottonwoods.

I noticed that Drover stayed upwind from me and kept his distance. That just goes to show what a crude instrument his nose was. He couldn't appreciate the coyote love potion, which was fine because it wasn't meant for jugheads like him.

Around noon, I altered course and turned south. We made our way through the under-

G.L. Holmes

brush and came out just below the ranch
house, a long cement building with a flat roof.

It was a good thing that I had already dis-
posed of Rufus. Otherwise I would have been
challenged at this point and would have been
forced to whip the ranch's number one guard
dog—not an impossible feat, by any means,
but it would have distracted me from my
primary mission.

Up ahead, in a wide grassy flat, I saw a dog.
My heart leaped with joy—until I realized it

was Plato, not Beulah. It appeared that he was out practicing his bird stuff—pointing, I guess they call it.

He was creeping through some tall grass, had his nose stuck out on one end and that long tail of his stuck out on the other, and he was paying no attention to ranch security.

I decided to give him a little thrill. I gave Drover the sign for "shut up and stay behind me" and we started sneaking up behind the bird watcher. Plato had just gone into his point and froze, with his tail throwed out like a stick, his ears cocked, and one front leg up in the air, when I walked up behind him.

"CHIRP!"

"Ahhhhhheeee!" His point fell apart, he flew in five different directions at once, squalled, and barked once as he headed for the house. He'd sprinted about fifteen yards when he figgered it all out, and then he came back.

"Oh, thank heaven it was you, Hank!"

"What did you think it was, a giant bird?"

"That thought did cross my mind, but my main concern was that Rufus might have come back on the place. He's an awful brute and often torments me when I'm out . . ." He lifted his nose and sniffed the air. "Do you fellows smell something dead? Or is it a skunk?"

"It's Hank," said Drover. "He's wearing some new perfume 'cause he came over here to . . ."

"I'll do the talking, Drover. You work on suffering."

"Oh. Okay."

"Well, thank heaven it's not a skunk," said Plato. "I simply refuse to get involved with those things and yet I feel so guilty when one comes on the place. Do you see my point?"

"Where's Beulah?"

"I beg your pardon? Oh, Beulah. Yes, I know where she is, but in all candor, Hank, I'm not sure . . ."

I showed him some fangs and let a growl rumble up from my throat. "Where is she?"

"Do I hear you saying that you want to see Beulah, is that it? My only point is that she might not want to see you, Hank, I'm sure you . . ." I growled again, louder this time. "Okay, I think we understand each other. You'll find her over by that big elm tree."

"Thanks."

"But I hope you'll try to understand my position, Hank."

I started walking off, but then I stopped. "Exactly what is your position?"

"Well, briefly stated, Hank, and taking it

one point at a time: number one, it appears to me that . . ."

"Never mind. We'll study on that some other time."

"That's fine, Hank. I'll be over here working out and if there's anything I can do, just let me know."

Plato went back to his bird-pointing and I headed for the elm tree. All at once I noticed that Drover was following me.

I told him to scram and go work on his character development.

"Oh Hank, just let me go over and say hello to Beulah."

"Promise you won't make a spectacle of yourself? You'll say hello and then get lost?" He promised. "Okay, just this once."

We trotted over to the tree. I didn't see her at first, but then there she was, over on the shady side, and mercy, my poor heart went off like a string of firecrackers! There was that fine collie nose, the perfect ears, the small brown eyes, the soft breeze blowing her flaxen hair.

I had to stop a minute to rest, and Drover, dang his soul, went streaking over to her. He started jumping up and down and spinning in circles.

"Hi Beulah, gosh you're so pretty I can

hardly stand it, I came all the way over here just to see you, I think I'm in love with you and if you think you might love me . . ."

It only took me a few seconds to restore order, once I got there, but by then the damage had already been done. Drover had made a fool of himself, and naturally that was a reflection on me. I growled him off and sent him on his way.

Then I turned to the lady of my dreams. "Hi, Beulah."

"Hello, Hank." Our eyes met and I knew that the old magic was still there. And in that honey-smooth voice of hers, Beulah said, "He's cute, isn't he?"

"Huh?"

"Drover's such a darling little . . ." Her eyes widened. She lifted her nose and moved her head in a half-circle. "Do you smell something?"

Heh, heh. I had her now. She would be putty in my hands.

"Yes, Beulah, and I can reveal its source. What you smell is an exotic love potion, known only to the wild coyote tribes and passed down from generation to generation since the dawn of time. Risking death and fates too horrible to mention in polite company, I stole the secret formula from a band of savage coyotes—and Beulah, I did it just for you."

"Oh Hank, you," she moved upwind, "you shouldn't have done that. Why, you might have been . . ."

"Killed? Maimed?" I moved upwind. "Dear lady, to die in your service would be an honor of which I am unworthy of which."

She scooted around upwind. Guess she was afraid of being overwhelmed. "But honestly, Hank, fighting coyotes! Why, they're very . . ."

"Dangerous? Deadly? Ferocious? Yes, my lady, all of those things." I slipped around upwind. "But with the memory of your lovely face etched on my heart, my only fear of death is that I might not see you again."

"Oh Hank, you do carry on, don't you?" She moved upwind.

"Yes, my dear lady. It isn't my usual nature to be loving and poetic." I moved upwind. "As you very well know, my years of combat and detective work have given me the outward appearance of steel, but beneath that shell of armor lie the gentler emotions known to ordinary dogs."

She got up and moved upwind. "Hank, are you feeling all right? You don't have a fever, do you?"

"Yes, I have a fever, Lady Fair, and I admit it without shame." I moved upwind. I mean, I had to give that perfume a chance to do its stuff. "It's a fever of the heart, and some people would even describe it as . . . LOVE!"

"Oh my, how . . . nice. But Hank, I must admit something to you." She got up and moved.

"I know what you're going to say, my petunia. How many tortured nights have I spent dreaming of the time you would say those words to me? Ach, there's no pain to compare with the ache of unblemished love!"

She moved upwind. "Hank, I don't know how to say this."

"Yes, my tulip, I have the same problem." I moved. "We spend so little time speaking the language of the heart that we find it hard to say those three simple words. Am I right, my perfect rose, three simple words?"

"Yes, Hank, three simple words, but . . ." She moved.

I moved. "Just say them, Beulah, out with them and we'll go plunging into the unknown!"

"All right, Hank, here goes: *You smell awful.*"

"HUH?"

She moved upwind. "I'm sorry, Hank, I wish I could think of a nicer way to put it, but you don't take hints. And I just can't relax and enjoy myself when I feel I'm sitting beside a skunk."

"Yes, I see. Then you might say that the magic perfume hasn't worked on you." She nodded. "Which might explain why you've been moving around so much." She nodded. "Almost as though you were trying to, well, stay upwind of me."

She gave me a sad smile. "I'm sorry, Hank. I know you went to a lot of trouble to get your secret potion, but it just doesn't work."

"That's bad news, Beulah. I was counting on it."

"But you don't need secret potions. What I like about you is *you.* Can't you see that?"

I hung my head. "No, I can't, I really can't. I mean, I'm such a big lunk. I'm awkward and clumsy. I never know what to say around a woman."

"I think you do very well."

"No I don't. My tang gets tungled when I try to talk to you and everything comes out wrong. And I know there are other dogs in the world who are much better looking."

"Now you stop talking that way!" She gave me a stern look. "You're talking about a good friend of mine. You're . . . well, maybe you are a little awkward sometimes, but I know you're sincere. And yes, maybe there are dogs with, uh, more refined manners and features, but in your own rough, country way, you have a certain, well, charm."

I studied on that for a minute. "You know, you're right, Beulah. I really do have a lot of charm, and I had it a long time before I tried rolling on a derned skunk."

"Yes but . . ."

"And one of the things I've always admired about you, my peach blossom, is that you look beneath the surface and find the fruit amidst the thorns, so to speak."

"But Hank, I must tell you . . ."

"Hush, my cactus flower, you needn't expose those fragile words to the hot winds of this unfeeling world."

"Hank, you had better listen . . ."

"I am listening, my prairie winecup, to the strains of a song that has been echoing through the corridors of my soul for many months. And now you will hear it, sung for the first

111

time by the dog who wrote it for . . . for his one and only true love."

She let out a sigh and gave me an odd smile. "Very well, Hank. If you wrote a song for me, the least I can do is listen to it."

CHAPTER

11

BEULAH'S SONG

I have the strangest dream, Beulah my
  dear,
I'm standing close to you and holding
  you near.
I feel electric shock, just being close by,
Touching your flaxen hair and seeing
  your eyes.

I don't understand this thing! Is it a
  lark?
I wake tossing and turning and yearning
  alone in the dark.
And hearing my bark again.

These feelings are strange to me, I can't
  explain

What makes me feel ten feet tall but
  brings me such pain.
It's bound to be sorcery, Beulah, my
  dove,
Some trick of the sleeping mind . . . or
  could it be love?

But I don't have time for love or poetry
  or song!
Protecting my ranch from dangerous
  forces, I've got to be strong!
But maybe I'm wrong again.

Beulah listened, wearing that same sad smile
on her lips. It seemed that a mist came over her
eyes, and then she sang to me:

Hank, you're a handsome dog, heroic
  and bold.
You're what we talk about when stories
  are told.
But heroes are restless ones, they're here
  and they're gone.
Their ladies wake up alone to greet the
  new dawn.

Plato is not like you, he's meek and
  refined.

Sometimes I think I should follow my
  heart instead of my mind!
But Plato is kind to me.

We sang the last verse together. Beulah sang
the part in the parenthesis.

Beulah, I pledge my heart (We can be
  friends)
To you this day (Very good friends)
I'll never leave you now (Plato is dear)
I've come to stay (Plato is near)

It's not just sorcery
Beulah, my dove
I'm not just dreaming now (You're only
  dreaming, Hank)
I'm sure I'm in love (You think you're
  in love).

Beulah took a deep breath and looked off in
the distance for a long time. "Hank, that was
a very nice song. I only wish things had
worked out differently for us."

It was pretty clear at this point that the song
had worked. I had made a small error in judg-
ment, rolling on the danged skunk, but I had
made up lost ground with the singing.

"Oh, we mustn't mourn over what-might-have-been. One nice thing about the past is that it's past. Now," I scootched over closer to her, "how about a little kiss for your favorite troubadour?"

"Oh, I guess . . . just a little one." She closed her eyes and leaned over. I waited to be touched by the branding iron of love. But all at once her eyes popped open and she made a terrible face. "Oh Hank, I can't kiss you when you smell like that!" She moved several steps away from me. "And I shouldn't be kissing you anyway. There's no sense in pretending."

"Huh? Well, hey listen, I can take a bath, if that's all you're worried about."

She shook her head. "No, it's more than that. Don't you understand? Hank, you're a fine dog. I admire you very much . . . in certain ways, and in another time and place . . . Hank, I'm pledged to another."

"Another *what*?"

"Another dog."

I felt I had just been hit over the head with a post. "I see. And I suppose that means Plato?" She nodded. "How could you choose a bird dog over a cowdog?"

She shrugged. "It just turned out that way. We don't always control the way we feel."

"Would it help at all if I challenged him to a fight to the death?"

"No, that would be childish, and it wouldn't change a thing."

"It's all coming clear now. I wasted my time, I wasted your time, I wasted my very best song. It's time for me to shove off and find something to fill this crater in my heart."

She looked away. When she turned back to me, there was a tear sliding down her long collie nose. "But Hank, you'll always be a special friend."

I got up to leave. "Thanks, Beulah. Since I plan to commit suicide, I probably won't be needing a friend, but I appreciate the offer."

"Oh Hank, don't be silly!"

I started walking away. "It'll be quick and painless, don't worry. I'll die with your face

on my mind, and then you won't have old smelly Hank to worry about any more. Good-bye, Beulah, goodbye forever."

I called to Drover and he came at a run. Plato saw me leaving. "Leaving so soon, Hank? I thought you might stay for supper."

"Plato, old buddy," I called out, "what I'd really like to do is have *you* for supper, but I guess that'll have to wait."

He nodded and waved. "Thanks, Hank, any time."

Drover caught up with me. "Where we going?"

"I'm going to join my ancestors, Drover."

"Oh. A family reunion?"

"Not exactly."

We headed up toward the house. I was going to cut through the yard and then strike out across country, but just then a pickup pulled up in front of the house and stopped. A man got out and went up to the door and knocked. He was carrying some radishes and onions.

It was the same Baxter fellow we had seen at the low-water crossing two nights ago, the guy who lived on the next ranch down the creek. And I had a suspicion that he might be hauling something interesting in the back of his pickup.

While he was talking to the lady at the house, Drover and I went over and sniffed out the pickup. Then we marked all four tires, just in case we might need to run a check on it later on.

I had just finished the back left tire when a freckled nose appeared above me. Directly above the nose, located at right angles perpendicular to the line of the nose, were two big brown eyes, one on each side.

They were pretty brown eyes, nestled below two long feathery lashes. "Hello again, big boy."

"Well blow me down, I believe it's Miss Scamper. Imagine meeting you twice in the same week!"

"This is your lucky day, you big old hairy thing," she said, batting her eyelashes. "What you got planned for the rest of the day?"

"Oh, I'd thought I might get run over by a truck, but, uh, I might could be talked out of that."

"Really? What would it take?"

I cleared my throat. "To be perfectly honest about it, Miss Scamper, not much."

"Well, just jump your big bad self up here and we'll go for a little ride, hmm?"

Drover had come around the back of the

pickup by this time and heard some of the conversation. "Hank," he whispered, "you better not. Beulah might see you."

I looked off toward the elm tree. Beulah was watching. "Yes, she might, Drover, but that's a chance I'll have to take. Stand back, son, I'm fixing to load up."

I coiled my legs and gave a mighty leap, clearing the tailgate and landing right on Miss Scamper.

"Oops, sorry ma'am. Hope I didn't hurt you."

She batted her lashes and grinned. "You're such a big old boy. And you jump so high. And I love your smell!"

"Yeah? I can already tell you have good taste."

She rubbed up against me. "What is it, if you don't mind telling?"

"It's a secret formula, ma'am, but I guess I can tell you."

"I guess you can."

"Dead skunk, specially aged and very rare."

"Ooooo! I love it."

Drover was still on the ground. "Hank, can I go?"

"No. Get lost. Go climb a tree."

I could hear his claws hitting the tailgate as

he tried to jump in. Then he got a hold with his front paws and scratched and clawed his way into the pickup. "I made it, Hank, you proud of me?"

I was all prepared to order him out, but then I heard Baxter walking back to the pickup. I figgered it would be best to lay low or he'd throw me out again. I laid low. He got into the cab, kicked off the motor, and started up the hill.

I went back to the tailgate and waved good-bye to Beulah. She had seen the whole thing, and when I waved she stamped her feet and yelled, "I don't care! Just go on with your little strumpet, because I don't . . . ohhhh!" She burst into tears.

"Well, I don't care either, so that makes us even!" I yelled back. "You had your golden opportunity and you messed up!"

Well, I'd gotten the last word on Beulah, but in the process of barking this message to her, I clean forgot about exposing myself to the driver. We'd just topped that big hill there in front of the house and crossed the cattleguard, when Baxter laid a heavy foot on the brakes. We came to a screeching stop.

He jumped out of the cab and looked in the back. "You dadgum dogs, get out of my pickup and go home! Hyah! Sooey!"

I glanced at Miss Scamper. She shrugged. "We have trouble staying together, don't we, big boy?"

I was fixing to answer when I got hit in the ribs with a bundle of bailing wire. Drover had already abandoned ship, and I figgered I'd better do the same before the storm got any worse.

"See you around, Miss Scamper."

"Come see me sometime," she said, waving goodbye.

THE RETURN OF THE GIANT RATTLESNAKE

I headed west at a good clip and it took Drover a while to catch up with me. "Where we going, Hank?"

"Back to the ranch, where do you think?"

"How can we do that when we swore an oath never to return?"

"Look, Drover, there are several different kinds of oaths: long term, short term, forever, and temporary. What we swore was your basic two-day oath."

"Oh. I didn't know that."

"And it's just about expired, so we need to get back to work."

"Well, that worked out about right, didn't it?"

"I try to figger things pretty close, son."

"But what about your family reunion?"

"I've decided there's no sense in joining my ancestors at this point, Drover. Why should I deprive my ranch and the world of one of its most valuable natural resources?"

"That's a good question."

We loped on down the creek, past the low-water crossing, and followed the caliche road on west. I was hoping we wouldn't meet up with Rufus and the coyotes, and sure enough, we didn't.

"Well, Drover, how did the suffering go? Did you work on your character development?"

"Sure did, Hank. Well, I tried, but you know what? While you were over there talking to Beulah, I got the feeling she was trying to make eyes at me. I kind of think she likes me, Hank."

I studied the runt to see if he was joking. He wasn't. "I guess in some ways it's a comfort to go through life with below-normal intelligence."

"Could be, Hank. We ought to ask her about it some time."

I decided to drop the subject. I mean, there's no sense in beating a dead horse with a sow's ear.

It was around four o'clock in the afternoon when we topped the last hill and looked down at ranch headquarters. Everything was just where we'd left it: the house, the yard, the machine shed, the gas tanks, the corrals, the saddle shed.

Made me feel good to see the old place again, in spite of the heavy responsibility that had already begun to settle upon my massive shoulders. Good or bad, it was my ranch.

"Well, Drover, there it is. The women may come and the women may go, but the ranch will always be the ranch. And look, there's little Alfred out in the yard, playing with his trucks. And Sally May has just walked out the door to check on him and . . ."

All at once, the peace and tranquility of the afternoon was shattered by a scream.

"What was that?"

Drover looked around. "Well, it sounded a lot like a scream."

Sally May was standing on the sidewalk, looking toward little Alfred and holding her hands up to her face. Pete the Barncat came creeping out of the flowerbed. He appeared to be stalking something, then suddenly he jumped back.

There was another scream. By this time I

had traced it to Sally May.

"Drover, it appears that we arrived just in time. Something's wrong down there and we'd better find out what it is. Come on."

We went flying down the hill. In situations like this, I go to DefCon Five and turn on maximum speed, which means that I become a blur of motion streaking across the pasture. Anything unfortunate enough to get in my way is broken, knocked aside, and sometimes even burned.

G. L. Holmes

When I had reached the driveway in front of the house, I met Pete. He had just shot through the fence and was looking for a tree to climb.

"That rattlesnake is back again," said Pete, "and he's mad enough to bite."

"What about the child?"

Pete was backing away. "He bites too, but it's the snake that worries me. You'd better do something, Hankie."

The word "snake" sent cold shivers down my back. Then I heard that awful buzz and saw the snake slithering into a coil, not more than five feet from Little Alfred. The poor kid was grinning and cooing, just didn't understand what was going on.

He took a step toward the snake. It struck at his hand but missed. Sally May stood nearby, too terrified to move.

The snake began to reload, drawing himself into another deadly coil. He buzzed, he flicked out his tongue, he glided into his coils.

Little Alfred made a happy sound and took a step toward the snake. Behind me, I heard Drover's voice. "Hank, what are you going to do?"

"I don't know if I've ever told you this, Drover, but I'm terrified of snakes."

He gasped. "Oh no, you can't be, Hank, not

at a time like this, somebody's got to do something!"

"I know, I know, but I just can't. That buzz . . . it does something to me, I can't move. You go, Drover. This is your opportunity."

"I would, Hank, but . . . well, my leg just went out on me and . . ."

The snake was coiled. He raised his head and cocked it back. Little Alfred giggled and took another step.

Before I knew what I was doing, I exploded and flew over the fence and started barking. The snake turned to me with his wicked eyes and flicked out his tongue. Little Alfred reached down to pick him up.

I had no choice.

I took two big leaps and landed right in the middle of the coils. That terrible buzzing filled my ears but I tried to shut it out. I pawed and I snapped and at last I got the snake in my jaws and gave it a shake. I felt something sting my right ear, but I tried not to think about it.

I knew I'd been bit and injected with a fatal dose of poison. I knew I had maybe five minutes left to live.

Sally May rushed over and swooped up the baby in her arms and carried him away. "Oh

Alfred, my baby, thank God you're safe!"

The fight didn't last long, once I got the snake in my jaws and started slinging him around. I mean, we're talking about jaws that can crush rocks and snap fenceposts in half, so a snake, even a big one, doesn't stand much of a chance.

It was a glorious moment of triumph. Sally May rushed over and hugged my neck. She cried and said I was the bravest dog in the world and apologized for all the tacky things she'd said about me.

I enjoyed it, even as the poison rushed through my body and my eyes grew dim. This was the way I'd always wanted it to end. It took the poison only a couple of minutes to reach my heart, and then

(EDITOR'S NOTE: On April 14, at approximately 5:32 Central Standard Time, Hank the Cowdog lost consciousness, went into convulsions, and slipped into a deep coma. Death followed shortly. Cause of death was determined to be a massive dose of poison from a six-foot diamondback rattlesnake.

One of the bravest dogs ever to

come out of the Texas Panhandle. Hank was loved and admired by everyone who knew him. At his funeral, Beulah the Collie collapsed in a paroxysm of grief and had to be carried from the scene. Miss Scamper the Beagle, another of Hank's female admirers, threw herself upon the body and asked to be buried with him.

Her request was denied on the grounds that if the authorities allowed her to be buried with the Hero, hundreds of other lady dogs in Texas would demand the same honor.

Burial was at the ranch, under the direction of Slim and High Loper. After the funeral, all livestock was driven from the 640 acre home pasture where the Hero was laid to rest. The home pasture has been dedicated as the Hank the Cowdog Memorial Park and will never be used to pasture livestock again.

"Taking a section of grass out of production was the least we could do in this situation," Loper remarked at the dedication of the new park. "What really hurts is that our Hank is gone.")

PLEASE TURN TO
NEXT PAGE

All right, I wrote that stuff about the funeral and all, and maybe I exaggerated a little bit. But it could have happened that way, very easily. No ordinary dog could have survived that rattlesnake bite. But I did.

I was all prepared to die, don't you see, but it just didn't happen that way. I guess cheating death had become such a habit with me that, even with a quart of deadly rattlesnake venom rushing through my veins, I couldn't die.

The part about convulsions and slipping into a coma, that was all true. I passed out and when I regained consciousness, I was lying on the kitchen table—in Sally May's house, if you can believe that.

Slim and High Loper were standing over me. Sally May stood off to one side, holding Little Alfred in her arms.

"I believe the old dog's going to make it," said Loper. "Good job, Hank."

I wagged my tail. It took considerable effort. You can't imagine what a bad effect two quarts of rattlesnake venom has on your tail muscles.

Slim bent down and studied my right ear. "Loper, it appears to me that the snake struck him on the tip of his ear and the fangs went all the way through. Look, you can see the fang marks."

Loper leaned over and looked at my ear. "Yup, sure looks that way."

Slim pushed his hat to the back of my head. "I don't believe the old rascal got a drop of poison."

Huh? Well, that was easy for *him* to say, since he wasn't the one who was lying there on the table, fighting for his life against half a gallon of deadly venom.

"Why do you reckon he passed out?"

Slim shrugged. "Probably fainted."

Loper looked over at Sally May. "Hun, he's all right. You want me to go ahead and give him the full treatment?"

She came over and stroked my head. "Let's do. He was so brave out there, he deserves it."

That sounded more like it. Sympathy is a wonderful medicine. And it just seems to be better when it comes from an admiring woman.

I didn't know what "the full treatment" was, but I had reason to suspect that it was going to be pretty good—warm milk over toast, eggs and milk, maybe even a big juicy steak.

Loper picked me up and carried me into another room. I just closed my eyes and enjoyed the ride. I could almost taste that steak.

You know what "the full treatment" was? A

DADGUM BATH! They throwed me into the bathtub and lathered me up with stinking perfumy soap. They picked fleas off my belly. They pulled ticks off my ears. They pulled cockleburs out of my tail. They pulled sandburs off my back.

Five minutes in that tub just about ruined me. Never mind the rattlesnake poison, I was worried about dying of cleanliness! I took it as long as I could, and then I said to myself, "I've got to get out of here."

I jumped out of the tub and tried to shake all that stuff off. Guess I throwed water everywhere, got Sally May so agitated that she yelled, "Get him out of here before he ruins the wallpaper!"

That was music to my ears. Loper pitched me out the back door. "Hank, I don't know how you do it, but I think you could find a way to screw up a bowl of ice cream."

I didn't hang around for my steak and eggs. I jumped the fence and made a wild dash for the sewer. I didn't bother to wade into that nice green pool of water. I flew into it.

And oh, it was so nice! How I love sewer water! It soothed me, it healed me, it brought back my deep manly smell. I give those healing waters full credit for counteracting the rattlesnake venom. It saved my life.

Well, I was rolling around in the water when Drover came along. "Oh Hank, I thought we'd lost you. Boy, am I glad to see you alive!"

"Alive and well, Drover. It takes more than a gallon of rattlesnake venom to put me out of commission."

"A whole gallon, no fooling?"

"Yes sir, injected directly into my juggling vein."

"Gosh, it's a miracle you survived. I almost died of fright, just watching."

"It's all in a day's work, Drover—fighting snakes, cheating death, courting women." I climbed out on dry land and gave myself a shake. "Now we'd better head for the gas tanks and get some shut-eye. In another three-four hours it'll be dark, and you know what that means."

Drover rolled his eyes around. "What does that mean, Hank?"

"Strange sounds in the night, creepy-crawly things, monsters, murders, another case for us to crack. There's no end to it, Drover."

We trotted over to the gas tanks and found our gunny sack beds just as we had left them. I fluffed mine up, walked around it three times, and flopped down. In seconds, I was asleep and dreaming about a big juicy bone.

"Hank?"

"Huh?"

"How come I can't quit thinking about Beulah?"

I cracked one eye. "It's a bad habit. It shows poor training and a lack of discipline. We don't have time for that nonsense. Now go to sleep."

"Okay." There was a moment of silence, then, "Hank, do you ever dream about Beulah?"

"I used to, but not any more. She chose Plato and I'm finished with her, forever. Go to sleep."

At last he was quiet. I drifted off to sleep again and went looking for that same juicy bone I'd been working on. I was floating along when all at once I saw . . .

Gosh, she was pretty, the long collie nose, the deep brown eyes, the long flaxen hair . . .